TAKE MURDER...

TAKE MURDER . . .

John Wainwright

ST. MARTIN'S PRESS
NEW YORK

10 9 8 7 6 5 4 3 2 1
First Edition

Library of Congress Cataloging in Publication Data

Wainwright, John William, 1921-
    Take murder.

    I. Title.
PR6073.A354T3   1981   823'.914   80-28485
ISBN 0-312-78357-4

THE BEGINNING

In the beginning was the law. A magnificent law. Some would argue, and with justification, the most perfect law the world had ever known.

The law was at once merciful and ruthless, magnanimous and awful in its might. It was a thing of exquisite checks and balances. It was as near to pure justice as any law had ever been.

It had, however, one flaw.

As near as dammit, it refused to acknowledge that it could be wrong.

ONE

Take murder . . .

It is now a crime; one more crime. Nothing unique. Since topping went out of vogue, it isn't even a special crime. It never really was; only the punishment was unique and, now that punishment has been abolished, murder has been slotted in amongst all the other crimes.

A form of theft, perhaps? The theft of a life? I've heard the argument and, in the hands of a good debater, it sounds a good argument. Good, that is, until it is examined. Examine it and certain important subsidiary questions crop up. For example . . . whose life? Of what value is that life? But if that life is valueless – other that is than to the owner of that life, who may value it for 'sentimental' and mawkish reasons – then the argument based upon the theft of life falls down. Anything without value is incapable of being stolen . . . basic Criminal Law. No value, no theft – no theft, no murder: an equally valid argument.

Not that the D.I. would have subscribed to that argument.

The detective inspector was known, almost revered, as a conscientious policeman. Tallboy; a man to whom law enforcement was a vocation. A man (I would say) blinded by an illogical code of ethics.

'A sad thing, Inspector.'

He voiced the words. Whether he meant them or not is debatable; he was – still is, I suppose – a man of simple emotions. The woman was dead . . . ergo it was 'sad'. That she was a dead whore of no consequence; that violence and even murder was, to her kind, almost an

7

occupational hazard was something he must have known, but chose to ignore.

I nodded, but remained silent.

'One o'clock,' Tallboy murmured.

I corrected him by saying, 'Shortly after one o'clock. I joined Constable Turnbull at one o'clock. Outside Barclays Bank. We walked, normal pace, down Elvin Street, then turned left. Turnbull spotted the shoe, that's how we found the body. Then I started the ball rolling.'

'You saw nobody?'

'Not a soul. Not even a car.'

Around us, the constables I'd called in from various beats stood in groups waiting for instructions. A Panda van and a squad car had parked about twenty yards from the body. There was the usual air of expectation; almost a comic-opera atmosphere. The 'gentlemen of the chorus' waiting with the two 'junior leads' for the entrance of the 'stars'. There was even what might be described as 'first-night nerves'.

Meanwhile, Tallboy and I stood about two yards from the body and, with the aid of torches, killed time by staring at the corpse and talking quietly together.

Tallboy said, 'She's dead, of course?'

'Quite dead. I allowed Turnbull to touch her . . . once. The carotid pulse. She's dead. Strangled, wouldn't you say?'

'Strangled,' agreed Tallboy. 'Manual strangulation at a guess.'

'It would seem so.'

An odd thing about the police machine; odd, because it places such a high priority upon the crime of murder. It is never actually *geared* for an immediate enquiry. That I find odd. A murder is committed and there is a time lapse. An hour, two hours – sometimes more – before the various sections of a force required to work together on a

8

murder enquiry can be gathered. The comparatively simple logistics are not pre-ordained; each murder starts from a zero; from the report or the finding of the body, and the standard procedure which follows every commission of this crime has to be built up from ground level, as if this was the first murder ever committed in the force area. This I find odd. Even stupid, although as a mere uniformed inspector the voicing of such opinions would have gone unnoticed. And perhaps still will.

I simply note that, in the early hours of that September morning, when Detective Inspector Tallboy and I stood guard on the body of the murdered prostitute, there was ample time for any killer to leave the scene and lose himself in the streets of Bordfield.

'Identity?' asked Tallboy.

'A professional whore. She works under the name of "Samantha". Her real name is Walters . . . Emilia Walters. She lives with another of her kind in a bed-sitter in Kale Court.'

Tallboy sighed and murmured, 'Poor bitch,' and I think he meant it.

One must assume that the wildly inaccurate musings of whoever was responsible for the amalgamation of police forces contained some germ of theoretical advantage. I have yet to find it, but it must be there, somewhere. From a practical point of view, amalgamation was a complete disaster; officers, whose whole service had been structured to a loyalty to a particular force, were suddenly asked to forget that loyalty and, instead become unimportant pawns in some vast, impossible-to-handle law-enforcement Goliath which, because of its very size, destroyed whatever 'personal touch' each individual force had enjoyed.

For myself, I had joined Bordfield City Police Force. I had worked my way up to the rank of uniformed inspector and, at the time of amalgamation, policed the Bowling Side Section of the Bordfield force. After we became a mere unit in the Lessford Metropolitan Constabulary I stayed at Bowling Side, kept my rank and (as far as *I* was concerned) remained an officer in the now defunct Bordfield City force. Tallboy was from the county force which had been caught up in the amalgamation and, from a personal viewpoint, was the only good thing to come from an otherwise ridiculous fusing-together.

We were of an age. Our tastes tallied in many ways; particularly when it came to music. He was married but without children, I was a confirmed bachelor living with my invalid mother; but this slight difference never interfered with our mutual companionship. We liked each other's company; I suspect he secretly disapproved of my lack of what he might have called 'the milk of human kindness', or perhaps he thought it was a façade, beneath which lay the usual marshmallow centre.

It matters not. We liked each other and talked not merely as equals, but also as friends.

As he lighted a cigarette he said, 'I don't envy you, Eddie.'

'Why?'

'Bowling Side. God, what a place to police.'

'It has its problems,' I admitted.

It had, too. It was a jumble of mean streets, courts and alleys. If, in this age of permissiveness, any city can be said to have a Red Light District, that district of Bordfield was within the Bowling Side boundary. We certainly had more than our fair share of street-women; they lived – sometimes in flats, sometimes in basements, sometimes in rooms of the rows of broken-down terrace houses – and hawked their wares along the badly lit pavements or in the sleazy public houses.

And they all had their own pseudonym. This one, for

example. 'Samantha.' A pathetic reaching out for glamour in a profession which no amount of glamour could ever make other than foul. But who could blame her? Who, in his right mind, would pay to copulate with an unclean creature called Emilia Walters?

'The road blocks?' asked Tallboy.

'They're up . . . or should be by this time. I asked them to be organised when I wirelessed in. When I asked them to notify you.'

'*We'll* be lucky,' murmured Tallboy.

'Quite,' I agreed.

By this time the gawpers were gathering. Men and women – worn-out hags of both sexes – who, via the grapevine of their kind, had learned of the build-up of police officers. Like sewer-rats sniffing some forbidden luxury, they edged their way into the mouth of the cul-de-sac. Silent, except for whispering among themselves. Frightened, but curious.

One of the night sergeants – a Sergeant Hobson – joined us.

He said, 'Inspector Caan. I think we'd better start getting some sort of crowd control organised.'

'I think so, too,' I agreed.

Tallboy said, 'Nothing, Sergeant. Whoever asks, nothing. Not what's happened. Not even the name. Nothing!'

'I'll see to it, sir.'

I waited until Hobson was out of earshot, then I smiled and said, 'You have great faith, Chris.'

'In what?' Tallboy looked puzzled.

'That they don't already know.'

'I don't see how.'

'Chris.' I chuckled at the simple artlessness of the man, and him a detective inspector. 'These people *invented* E.S.P. Nobody tells them a damn thing, but they always know. Already they'll know it's murder. Already they'll know the name of the victim. They might even know the name of the murderer. They won't share that knowledge. But, take it from me, they already know more than we know.'

'Bowling Side.' The words were almost a sigh, and he shook his head in mock-despair as he spoke them.

'An evil place, Chris.' I did not raise my voice, I put no emphasis on any word, but I hoped he believed me. I said, 'We police it. We go through the motions. But we never get to the bottom . . . or ever will. This place, especially this square mile or so between the canal and Lessford Road, is well beyond hope. We patrol it, no more. We don't police it. We *daren't* police it. It would have our throat out if we tried.'

Tallboy grinned and said, 'You're one hell of a pessimist.'

'No. A realist. I do what I can – all I can – but I'm aware of my limitations.'

By dawn things were moving.

No, I must be more precise. The expression 'things were moving' is a gross over-simplification of the facts. The *police* were moving. The law-enforcement machine was beginning to turn. The various 'specialist services' – the forensic-science liaison crowd, the photographers, the sketch-planners, the qualified doctor required to pronounce life extinct – had all been and gone. The body was on a slab in the public mortuary, awaiting the arrival of the pathologist and a post-mortem examination.

Harris, the A.C.C. (Crime) for Bordfield Region, had visited the scene, if only to impart official blessing from on high. Chief Superintendent Lennox – Regional Head of C.I.D. – had also arrived and was still with us. My own uniformed superintendent – Superintendent Warlock – was also there, and with him Chief Inspector Perkins.

The place was crawling with all sorts and conditions

of men and women, all police officers. The narrow streets were choked with as fine a collection of police vehicles as one could wish for.

Lennox, Warlock, Perkins, Tallboy, P.C. Turnbull and myself grouped ourselves in a sheltered corner, away from the now considerable gaping crowd and clear of the bustle of non-activity being put on as a show by an increased number of uniformed and plain-clothes officers. Theoretically a 'search' was in progress. A search for what? Nobody knew. Nobody could even make an informed guess. Manual strangulation precluded any possibility of a weapon, but standard tactics at the start of a murder enquiry insisted that a thorough search be made of the area around where the body is found and standard tactics were being followed. An equally forlorn hope was 'house-to-house enquiries' – especially in the Bowling Side district – but I had no doubt that this equally standard practice would, in the near future, be solemnly organised.

Meanwhile Lennox was holding forth.

Lennox.

Working on the assumption that a police force can afford to include within its ranks a small quota of eccentrics, Lennox was acceptable. Just. His figure was Falstaffian, his head was as bald as an egg with whispy strands flying unhindered just above the ears, and his dress was of the mode favoured by stand-up comics of the old Music Hall days. And yet only the rawest recruit ever laughed at Lennox; in very little time it was learned that external appearances were never more deceptive – indeed, at a guess, he deliberately exaggerated those appearances – and under the obese and clownish shell lived a man who, in his own lifetime, had become something of a local legend in the matter of crime detection.

Lennox lent himself to underestimation, and that itself was one of his strengths.

He was discussing the possible situation of an 'Incident

13

Centre' or 'Operations Room' or, as it was once more bluntly named, a 'Murder Headquarters' . . . the police force, too, suffers from the present-day ailment of self-imposed ambiguity.

'The local nick,' he suggested.

'No room, I'm afraid.' Warlock shook his head. 'It's a purpose-built police station, sir. Functional.'

'Right.' Lennox sniffed. 'Let's make the bloody place function.'

The exchange merely accentuated a known pattern; Warlock's smooth and barely concealed dislike for Lennox's blunt disregard of polite protocol, and Lennox's cheerful don't-give-a-damn attitude concerning who or how many people liked *or* disliked him.

Chief Inspector Perkins murmured, 'The – er – the Recreation Room, sir?'

'I hardly think . . .' began Warlock.

'Why?' interrupted Lennox.

'The equipment.'

'Is it set in reinforced concrete?' asked Lennox innocently.

'Well – er – no. But . . .'

'Superintendent Warlock, old cock.' I saw Warlock visibly cringe at the 'old cock' addendum. Lennox continued, 'There's a lass on the slab. Dead. Strangled by the look o' things. From what I'm told she was a good-time type. A naughty girl. Even so, she's a damn sight more important than a ping-pong table. At least I think so, and what *I* think matters. C'mon. Let's have a decko at this Recreation Room.'

The Bowling Side Section Police Station's Recreation Room became the 'Incident Centre'.

To call it a victory for Lennox would be to overstate what was little more than a mild skirmish and a minor clash of personalities. The Recreation Room was the obvious, indeed the *only*, choice. Warlock's objection had (or so it seemed to me) been a token attempt to establish the right to determine what went on in his division; Kemington Division was his bailiwick and Bowling Side Section was part of that Division and – as always happened – when Regional Headquarters descended it became necessary to send out subtle reminders that, come the end of whatever case the higher echelon happened to be interested in, when they returned to Regional Headquarters Warlock was still divisional superintendent, and would be required to re-establish any authority they might have undermined.

Warlock had made his point.

But the table-tennis equipment had been folded up and stored away in a spare cell, and extra tables and chairs had been installed. The Post Office had agreed to provide at least one additional telephone and Regional Headquarters promised typewriters, typists and recording equipment in order to cut down on the time needed to build up a file on whatever facts and evidence we might glean.

By this time it was mid-morning; the movement was ponderous, but there *was* movement.

Lennox said, 'Right. Normal enquiries under way. We need somebody with local knowledge.'

Warlock – perhaps as some small retaliation for the chief's inspector's original suggestion of the Recreation Room as an Incident Centre – said, 'Inspector Caan, you've been here . . . seven years, isn't it?'

'Just over seven years,' I agreed.

'Move into plain clothes,' said Warlock. 'Chief Inspector Perkins can cover the administrative side of the section from subdivision.'

Perkins looked less than pleased.

15

But Lennox wobbled his chins in agreement and said, 'Fine. Fine. Tallboy and Caan. Work together, lads. A roving commission . . . see? Try to get back here each evening. Between eight and nine. I'll be here . . . we can compare notes.'

Which is how it began.

It was the sort of arrangement only a man like Lennox would have approved, much less instigated. The house-to-house rigmarole would, of course, be gone through. The stodgy, uninspired routine of the standard murder enquiry would blunder its way forward, and the press and the public would be duly awed by the sheer weight of paper and the apparent limitless patience of officers who, if the truth were told, were bored to tears.

But this (as I saw things) was to be the combined P.R.-exercise-cum-long-stop. Lennox was deliberately making Chris and me the cutting edge of the *real* enquiry. Chris, because he was a fine detective; me, because I knew Bowling Side. Together because Lennox knew we were friends and would not, therefore, be out for individual kudos.

We left the police station and, in order that I might have a quick shave and change out of uniform, we rode to my house in Chris's car. On the way we discussed tactics.

'Food,' said Chris firmly. 'No enquiry benefits from an empty stomach.'

'There's a café,' I suggested. 'It's not quite "all night". The proprietor snatches a few hours of sleep, usually well after midnight. The prostitutes use it for snacks. And the pimps. Chips-with-everything . . . that sort of place.'

'It'll do.'

'Henry – the proprietor – he's not quite a copper's nark, but he's been known to drop hints. He knows most things.'

'I know the type.'

'It's as good a place as any, as a starting point.'
'Okay. That's where we start,' agreed Chris.

These cafés. They really are nauseous. The local government health officials could, without doubt, close them down; certain it is their standards of hygiene are light years below what the law demands. But they serve a purpose, and to close one down would merely ensure that another equally disgusting eating-place would crop up to cater for the same custom.

I presume it boils down to the old-old story . . . better the devil you know than the devil you don't.

Henry's café; one presumes it once had a name other than 'Henry's Place' by which it was universally known, but if so that name had long been forgotten. It had a stench peculiar to itself; a compound of burning fat, stale food, old cigarette smoke and general body filth. Vermin, too, perhaps . . . and cats. There was a preponderance of cats, none of them doctored, none of them spayed, therefore there was also a preponderance of kittens.

Henry (as he would tell anybody who asked) was a 'cat lover'. This meant they could fornicate and drop their never-ending litters as they pleased in and around his premises. If this was 'loving' cats, he spoke no less than the truth. Indeed, there was a certain feline slyness about the man himself. No movement was unnecessary and when he did move it was with a curious, silent manner. Even his speech had a certain sibilant purr; like an alley cat wishing to strike up temporary friendship with a stranger in order that it might be left in peace.

'Nothing, sir,' he said.

'Nothing?' Chris chewed at his sandwich as he asked the question.

Before Henry could answer I said, 'You cater for whores.'

'I don't ask questions, Mr Caan.'

'It wasn't meant to be a question.'

'Oh!'

We leaned on the filthy, lino-topped counter, sipped disgusting tea from chipped mugs, chewed our way through what purported to be 'cheese sandwiches' and asked questions. Behind us two men sat at the scattering of tables. Roadsters at a guess; certainly unemployed and unemployable. They, too, drank tea as a means of killing time.

'You've heard about it, of course,' said Chris.

'Somebody murdering Samantha?'

'Emilia Walters,' I corrected him. 'This is a murder enquiry. We dispense with stage names.'

'Yes . . . I've heard.' The admission was made with some reluctance.

Chris said, 'She was a prostitute.'

'I've already said. I don't ask . . .'

'Don't be so damn stupid,' I cut in. 'She was a slag. A whore. It's why she was murdered.'

'Is it?' Henry put on an expression of surprised interest.

'Any other reason?' asked Chris.

'I dunno.'

'An opinion, perhaps?'

'I don't have opinions, sir.'

I said, 'Why?'

'They can be very dangerous.'

'Clamming up,' said Chris, 'can be equally dangerous. More dangerous sometimes.'

'I wouldn't know.'

'Is there anything you *would* know?' I asked sarcastically.

'Not a lot.' Henry smiled. A cat's smile; a very knowing smile.

'The dead woman.' Chris tasted his tea.

'What about her?'

'You knew her. Knew her well enough to know her working name. Samantha. Did she use this place?'

'Sometimes.'

'Sometimes?'

'Often,' I suggested.

'Fairly often,' admitted Henry.

'How often?' asked Chris.

'Three – maybe four – times a week.'

'So you knew her?' I pressed.

'Mr Caan...'

'You *knew* her?'

'As well as I know any of 'em.' Very hastily he added, 'But that doesn't mean a lot.'

Men like Henry. I make no apology, I despised them and still do. They batten upon the offal of humanity. Street-walkers, petty law-breakers, scoundrels, ne'er-do-wells – people incapable of making even the simplest of meals – provide men like Henry with a fair-to-moderate living. They provide a bolt-hole, a temporary resting-place, for the subnormal stratum of every city's population.

Chris had more patience than I; born, no doubt, from years of interviewing morons of a like kind. Myself? I was rapidly becoming angry with this devious creature. Nor did I see the need to hide my anger.

I snapped, 'In case it hasn't penetrated that thick skull of yours, this is a murder enquiry.'

'I know.' Henry blinked at the change of tone. 'It's just that...'

'Questions are being asked. Being foxy can land you in trouble. Real trouble.'

'I'm not being...'

'The hell you're not!'

In a quieter voice Chris said, 'What was she like?'

'She was . . .' Henry rubbed his lips together to moisten them. 'Like you say. She was on the game. Past her best.'

'How old?'

'Thirty-ish. Maybe nearer forty.'

'And?'

'Look, mister, she wasn't bad. Generous. I've known her . . .'

'Don't,' I interrupted, 'feed us the whore-with-a-heart-of-gold line. It's hackneyed.'

'It's true, Mr Caan.'

'She had a friend,' said Chris.

'Lots o' friends, sir.'

'I mean one she lived with.'

'Oh, aye.' Henry nodded. 'Carlotta.'

'Oh, my God!' I murmured.

'That's what she likes being called, so that's the name I use.'

'Her real name?' asked Chris.

'I dunno. I never ask.'

'You are,' I said, 'a great one for minding your own business.'

'Aye, it pays round here.'

'Not on a murder enquiry,' I reminded him.

There was a pause in the questioning. These pauses are necessary; they enable the interviewer to correlate whatever answers have been obtained and from them determine the next series of questions to be asked. To separate the wheat from the chaff; the truth from the lies. To remind himself of the tiny contradictions and, from these contradictions, encourage a genuine lie, which in turn can be used as a lever via which to uncover the truth.

Chris lighted a cigarette and continued the questioning. I contented myself with watching Henry's face, and from his expression trying to pick out the lies.

'She used this place?' said Chris.

'Samantha?'

'We'll call her that if you like.'

'Yes, she came here sometimes.'

'Fairly often. That's what you said.'

'All right. Fairly often.'

'Alone?'

'Not always.'

'With a friend?'

'Sometimes.'

'Male or female?'

'Both.'

Chris leaned fractionally farther across the counter and said, 'Don't bugger me around, boy. You know *exactly* what I mean. With a man friend? With a customer?'

'I – er – I reckon.'

'Last time?'

'I – er . . .' Henry looked worried.

'The last time she came in here with a man?' repeated Chris.

'Last night.' The answer was little more than a whisper.

'Time?'

'I dunno.'

'What time were they in here?' snapped Chris.

'About – I dunno, maybe nine o'clock. Maybe a bit later.'

'For how long?'

'Half an hour . . . about.'

'Then they left?'

'Aye.' Henry nodded.

'Together?'

'Aye, of course together. You don't think . . .'

'I think,' said Chris, 'that if the man was a customer – and if he left with her – he hadn't at that time got what he'd paid for.'

'Oh!'

'I also think we'd better have some more details. Real details.' Chris took his notebook and a ballpoint from an inside pocket. He said, 'We'll start at the beginning. When they came in. Where they sat. What they ordered. What they said. When they left. Then a full description of the man . . . everything.' He smiled a frost-rimmed smile and added, 'Always bearing in mind you might be describing the murderer.'

'Oh, my Christ.'

'Now . . . we've all the time in the world, Henry.'

A good detective (and Chris Tallboy was – still is – a good detective) must, I suppose, have the patience of a Crow Indian. 'All the time in the world.' I think Chris did not use that expression lightly; slowly sometimes gently, sometimes threateningly, he pumped Henry dry of every ounce of possible information. It was, of course, a waste of time. The miserable creature knew very little. To an extent – to a very limited extent – he knew the life-style of the dead whore. He knew the handful of fellow street-walkers she counted as 'friends'. He knew the name of her pimp, her 'minder' . . . a disgusting Asian to whom she paid some percentage of her daily takings in return for being allowed to hawk her wares in comparative peace.

The man who'd been with her in the café the previous evening? His name, so Henry said, was Alfred. Just Alfred . . . an absence of surname ensures some degree of anonymity. He was, according to Henry, something of a 'regular'; some pathetic creature requiring to purchase his lust at fairly regular intervals.

The description of Alfred meant nothing. What it was fitted at least twenty per cent of the male population of Bordfield and more than twenty per cent of them wore the type of clothes the man had been wearing.

What I hadn't realised – what I *should* have realised

as a police officer responsible for the district – was that Henry's café was used as an unofficial 'headquarters' by many of the local street-women. I tucked that tiny piece of information away for future reference.

Chris finally closed his notebook and ended the prolonged, but near-barren session by saying, 'Right, son. Bowling Side Police Station. Some time within the next twenty-four hours. Tell 'em who you are and that we sent you. You'll be given a microphone and a cassette recorder. Everything. Everything you've told me. Everything you know about her. Anything else you might remember . . . it doesn't matter how unimportant it might seem. Chronological order, if possible, but that's not too important. Everything! That's what matters. We'll get a statement typed. Then you read it, sign it and the chances are you can forget we ever saw you.'

When we were outside the café I added, 'Unless, of course, he was the last person to see her alive.'

'Unless,' agreed Chris. As we climbed into the car he added, 'If that is so – if he *was* the last person to see her alive – we're up the creek.'

'I don't follow.'

Chris started the car and drove as he explained.

'Nine o'clock . . . thereabouts. That's when she was with Alfred in the café. One o'clock, thereabouts. That's when you and Turnbull found her. Four hours. Take thirty minutes off for the time they were in the café. Three hours, thirty minutes. Take the odd thirty off, just to give us room for mistakes. Three hours. Not the proverbial "short time". Not a quick bang in some dark alley. So if it's Alfred, it means a bed somewhere. And a bed points to somebody else seeing 'em, after they'd left the café.'

'And if you're wrong?' I asked. 'If it's a "short time".'

'Dunno.' He frowned his concentration. 'In the cul-de-sac where she was found. But that doesn't quite fit.

23

Rigor mortis hadn't set in, so that means a lot later than nine-thirty.'

'Not the mysterious Alfred,' I said gently.

'Not unless he's a glutton for punishment. Two "short times" in less than three hours.'

'And from the same slag.'

'Quite. If he *is* something of a stallion, why not go in for variety?' Chris blew out his cheeks in mock-disgust. 'Christ! What a way to live? Come to that, what a way to *earn* your living?"

'The oldest profession,' I reminded him.

'Well paid, too, except of course for bastards like Abdul Abulbul Emir.'

Our next call was at the home address of the dead woman; our next interviewee, 'Carlotta', the dead woman's room-mate.

I will not bore you with the details nor even with details of the stench-ridden hovel they called 'home'. Suffice to say that any self-respecting beast of the field would have walked away from the place.

'Carlotta' – her real name was Bertha something-or-other and her Birmingham accent was thick enough to cut with a knife – was less helpful than Henry the café pro-prietor. She knew nothing. She cared less.

Yes . . . she'd lived with the dead woman; they'd shared the cost of the place for about two years.

No . . . she didn't know much about the dead woman; they weren't friends – not what you could call friends – more like acquaintances.

Yes . . . she used Henry's place, sometimes; so did all the girls; it was a known pick-up spot.

Alfred? Alfred who? Alfred what? Half the men who paid for sex gave their wrong names anyway; girls who asked too many questions didn't get many customers.

Yes . . . beds were available for long sessions; paid for by the hour, night or day; some of the biddies, too old for the game, ran a nice side-line in rooms with beds.

No . . . she didn't know which bed the dead woman might have used; any of a score of beds; you got a customer willing to pay for something special, you took him to the nearest room.

Those were the type of answers; answers to be expected from a slut. To her, immorality was a business proposition. Something to be bought and sold on the open market. Dirt in a very tattered package.

Throughout the questioning she hardly looked up. She sat on a soiled divan and, to her, the painting of varnish on her fingernails was far more important than the filth of which she was a part. Far more important than that one of her kind had been strangled.

At the end of the interview Chris said, 'We'll need a statement.'

'Not from me, buster.'

'For God's sake! This is a murder enquiry.'

'I didn't murder anybody.'

'It could have been you,' I reminded her coldly.

'So?' She smiled. 'I live to screw another day. Ain't I lucky?'

'Why no statement?' asked Chris patiently.

'Well, I'll tell you.' This time she smiled at him. 'I make a statement. I say who I am, what I am. Nice . . . eh? Some bleedin' flatfoot wants a quick court trip. It's *there*. Signed and everything. Buster, it's a hard enough life without you creeps.'

Chris said, 'And if I promised you immunity?'

'I'd tell you where to stuff your immunity.'

In effect that was the end of the interview. Chris tried; he tried very hard. But these women have no sense of shame. No sense of moral obligation. Friendship means little to them. Civic duty means less. I was sickened as we walked back to the car.

Chris shrugged as we drove away. He said, 'You win some. You lose some.'

'We haven't got far,' I countered.

'We're doing fine.' He steered the car towards a less sleazy district of Bordfield. 'We're stirring things up. Word'll get round. One of them – with luck more than one – will come to *us*. They're scared, Eddie. Don't let the top-dressing fool you. Being scared goes with the profession. When one of them gets *too* scared . . . she'll come to us.'

We had our first real meal of the day at my home. Aunt Elizabeth (who lived with us and helped me look after my invalid mother) was one of the few genuine *Cordon Bleu* cooks not professionally employed and, before progressing to our interview with the 'Carlotta' woman, I'd telephoned home and arranged an approximate time of arrival.

Aunt Elizabeth had excelled herself. She had, I suspect, a rather silly old-maidish 'crush' on Chris; it amused me to watch her dithering around, ensuring that he ate and enjoyed everything.

The four of us – mother, Aunt Elizabeth, Chris and myself – talked as we ate and, quite naturally, the conversation centred on the murder of the street-woman.

The home-made potted shrimps were the *hors d'œuvre*. Delicious; fresh shrimps and best butter.

Mother said, 'Well, have you made progress, Edmund?'

Strange. I was 'Eddie' to everybody else in the world; even to Aunt Elizabeth. I'd been 'Eddie' to my father when he was alive. But to my mother I was 'Edmund'. I think the first time Chris heard it, it came as something of a surprise; at a guess he'd always thought 'Eddie' was short for 'Edward', but no: 'Edmund'.

26

I said, 'A little progress. Chris seems to think more than a little.'

'Christopher?'

My mother switched her attention.

'Enquiries are continuing, Mrs Caan, to coin a phrase.' Chris smiled one of his slightly twisted smiles. Gentle, but with a touch of sardonic worldliness. 'We aren't dealing with too intelligent a person.'

'You know that already?'

'He's a murderer,' said Chris simply.

'Does that follow?' I frowned as I asked the question. 'He's a killer, therefore he's a fool?'

'Foolish enough to think he can get away with it,' said Chris.

'Some have,' I reminded him. 'The Ripper, for example. And others less gruesomely inclined.'

'One murder, Eddie.' Chris chuckled. 'The first full day of enquiries. For Heaven's sake, don't blow it up into a Ripper case.'

'I'm sorry. It was just a passing thought.'

For the main course we had veal *chasseur*; fresh veal (Aunt Elizabeth was, I knew, the scourge of the local butcher) prepared in sherry, tomato and mushrooms, with creamed potatoes, asparagus tips and *sauté* onions. A meal for a king. (As far as Aunt Elizabeth was concerned, a meal fit for a detective inspector.)

The conversation continued, opened out a little.

Aunt Elizabeth said, 'A man? You seem to have little doubt about that, Inspector Tallboy.'

'Manual strangulation, Miss Caan.' Chris smiled. 'I can't remember any case where that method was used by a murderess.'

'As a personal opinion,' murmured mother, 'I would have thought the silly Women's Liberation Movement would have done their utmost to remove *that* particular anomaly by this time.' A look of mild disgust crossed her face as she added, 'They will, Christopher. Mark my words, they will.'

Chris smiled and said, 'It's a thought.'

'I fear it's a fact.'

'Mother,' I explained, 'holds some rather strange views on the subject.'

'Please don't apologise for me, Edmund.'

'No. I wasn't . . .'

'You could be right, Mrs Caan.' Chris, as always, eased us away from an argument. He said, 'Changing fashions. Even in crime. We have to keep abreast with things.'

We ate in silence for a few moments, then Mother said, 'Prostitutes, Christopher. What is the police attitude to them? I've asked Edmund, but he won't give me a complete answer.'

'There is no complete answer,' said Chris. 'They're there. We have to accept them.'

'As a necessary evil?'

'As – er – necessary. All men aren't like me – happily married. All men aren't like Eddie – born bachelors.'

'I may surprise you one day,' I smiled.

'Necessary, but not evil.' Mother pinned Chris down to a specific opinion.

'Mrs Caan . . .' Chris moved his fork a little as an aid to his explanation. 'Drink. It's necessary – even social – in moderation. In excess it's a disgusting thing. An evil, perhaps. Gambling – the same. An occasional flutter harms nobody. A similar argument can be put forward in favour of prostitution.'

'I don't think so.'

'Not a *good* argument,' conceded Chris.

'We're talking about human bodies being purchased for lewd purposes.'

28

'Hannah!' Aunt Elizabeth was shocked at the bluntness of Mother's remark.

'We are also,' said Chris slowly, 'talking about a basic human requirement.'

'A basic *male* requirement.'

Chris smiled tolerantly.

'You don't agree?' demanded Mother.

Chris said, 'I don't agree with murder, Mrs Caan. Like Eddie I handle law, not morals. The morals of the dead woman were – as you say – not what they should have been. But, whatever they were, they didn't merit her being strangled. Strangulation – not prostitution, ma'am – that's what the enquiry's about.'

I found it necessary to apologise for my mother. My mother of all people! Chris had been a guest in our house; a guest and a personal friend. I knew what Mother felt. I was aware of her intractable stand against any form of immorality and, to a great degree, I sympathised with her. But Chris *had* been a guest and (or so it seemed to me) she should have either steered clear of the subject or allowed Chris's view to go unchallenged.

Somewhat stumblingly, therefore, I apologised for her behaviour.

Chris chuckled and waved my attempts at apology aside. 'She's right,' he said. 'By her yardstick – by most people's yardstick – Emilia Walters got little more than she deserved. In the Old Testament days she'd have been stoned to death . . . *and* by law-abiding citizens.' As we climbed into the car he added, 'The next one. That's the real nasty bastard. Abdul Abulbul Emir. You know his real name, by the way?'

'Nayudu. Tomba Nayudu. Naturally he's called "Tommy". I think he's Indian, although he claims to be from Pakistan.'

'You know him?' Chris started the car.

'*Of* him.' I fiddled with the seat belt. After the meal I felt slightly over-fed; that comfortable feeling from which, if the circumstances allow, an armchair snooze can be born. I said, 'Rumours. He steers clear of trouble. The Race Relations people use him as a go-between some-times.'

'They have nice friends,' grunted Chris as he steered the car towards Bowling Side.

'He has influence. It can be useful.'

'But you don't know him? Personally?'

'No.' I hesitated, then added, 'There's gossip . . . the usual thing. His – er – credentials might not stand up to too severe a scrutiny.'

'An illegal immigrant in other words?'

'Just rumours,' I murmured.

'Eddie, why the hell aren't they jumped on?' There was a tetchiness about the question. Perhaps, after all, he'd been offended by Mother's dogmatic remarks. He said, 'They can be slammed. The bastards come here. Set up shop. Break the bloody law . . . and nobody does a damn thing. Some token arrest somewhere. Half a dozen, maybe. Once every few weeks. And – dammit – those they *do* arrest aren't the scum we want rid of. Some pathetic family . . . as a gesture. But the bastards – the *real* bastards – aren't touched. They go into business . . . this sort of business. Hawking dope. Jesus Christ! They shouldn't even *be* here. But nobody touches 'em. Why?'

'The Immigration Authority . . .' I began.

'The police,' he snapped. 'You. Me. Once they're here – once they're established – we're the people responsible, and we don't do a damn thing. Why?'

'It's – er – it's the colour thing,' I said.

'That,' growled Chris angrily, 'is the most wishy-washy excuse of 'em all. The bent bastards are bent bastards, and if they're polka-dot they're *still* bent bastards. All the various anti-colour-bar set-ups – okay, that's fine. Equality. Sure – equality, but top and bottom. The law hasn't any eyes, Eddie. It can't see the colour of a man's skin. Keep it that way. That's all I'm saying. All dogs aren't black . . . okay. But also all blacks aren't angels. Let's not forget that either.'

The outburst came as a surprise; the depth of feeling in the words. He was, I suppose, voicing the feelings of most policemen, but it seemed to be very deep, very bitter. I would hesitate to use the word 'prejudice' because that was what it was *not*. Indeed it was anti-prejudice, but from all angles.

A criminal was a criminal was a criminal, that's what he was saying. And who could argue?

But Tomba Nayudu was in for a hard interview.

The house was a semi-detached; a house in one of the very few rows of such houses in the Bowling Side district. The usual thing: a tiny front garden, a garage at the side and the upper storey pebble-dashed. The sort of house seen by the thousand in any middle-class area of any city, but almost unique in Bowling Side.

We'd arranged it. Chris would do the talking. I'd be corroborative witness to anything self-condemnatory Nayudu might say. I had this feeling that Chris was out to nail Nayudu. Not for the murder. For *anything*.

A teenage coloured girl answered the ring.

Chris said, 'Tomba Nayudu. Is he at home?'

The girl gave a tiny bow and said, 'I will see,' and made to close the door.

'He's at home.' Chris pushed the door wider. 'You'd know if he was out, without looking.'

The girl looked frightened, but stood aside as we entered.

31

Chris closed the door and said, 'Okay, pet. Lead the way.'

The outside of the house belied what was inside. Just about everything was expensive. No real taste, you understand. Far too much and far too many. Nayudu believed in displaying his wealth until it was almost overwhelming.

The girl led us into what was the front room. Deep, brocaded armchairs; thick-piled carpet; a five-bar electric fire; wall-lighting; the sort of wallpaper you have to pay the earth for; velvet curtains at the window; leather-covered ottomans. Again, too much and too many.

Nayudu was wearing a silk dressing-gown over twill slacks. He had a silk scarf tied at his neck. As we entered the room he lowered a copy of the *Purbodesh* and, from the comfort of one of the armchairs, looked annoyed.

He began, 'My girl, I thought I told you . . .'

'Forget what you told her,' snapped Chris. 'You have enough problems worrying about what you're going to tell us.'

Nayudu dismissed the girl with a wave of the hand. As Chris strolled farther into the room Nayudu said, 'You?'

'Us in general, me in particular.'

'Ah!' Nayudu smiled a smile which was a long way from a smile and murmured, 'Police.'

'Alas, for our sins.' Chris unbuttoned his mac. 'My colleague, Inspector Caan. I'm Detective Inspector Tall-boy.'

'I'm pleased.' Nayudu nodded a show of welcome. 'I am happy that you . . .'

'Why the hell should you be happy?' Chris stood straddle-legged, and pushed his hands into the pockets of his open mac. 'Why the hell shouldn't you be worried? Or if not worried, concerned?'

'Inspector, I assure you, I have nothing to be . . .'

'By God, you *have*.' Chris, it would seem, was going

32

to refuse the coloured man the right to end a sentence. 'One of your girls, "Samantha", was strangled last night. You have things to be worried about Nayudu.'

'One of *my* girls, Inspector. I assure you . . .'

'I assure *you*, you're a pimp. Let's start from there.'

The smile remained fixed, as Nayudu said, 'That is a most serious accusation to . . .'

'I'm not accusing you, I'm *telling* you. Keep saying "No" and we'll need a court to prove which one of us is a liar. Follow?'

'I . . .' Nayudu hesitated, then, still smiling, said, 'I am an ignorant Indian, sir. I don't . . .'

'An Indian.' Chris took a hand from its pocket and lifted the periodical Nayudu had been reading. 'An Indian, reading a Bangladesh magazine. 'What else are you, Nayudu, other than a liar?'

The smile left the coloured man's face. He said, 'Inspector, I think . . .'

'Don't think. Just listen.' Chris tossed the magazine back onto Nayudu's lap. 'What we can prove. *Prove* . . . okay? A woman was strangled to death last night. She worked under the name of "Samantha". She was a whore. Her real name was Emilia Walters. She had a "minder". A pimp. You! That much we can prove. What we can't prove – *yet* – is that you killed her or that you're an illegal immigrant. But, stay coy, and we'll have a damn good try at proving both those things. Those are the cards, Nayudu. Now, which game do we play?'

That was how the interview started. Chris set the pace and the coloured man hated him with his eyes. Not with his mouth; his words were as smoothly spoken as ever. Mock-reasonable words. Words with which he had flattered ignorant and frightened women. And, perhaps, ignorant and frightened men. Words with which . . .

TWO

My apologies...

The interview with Nayudu. It would be a waste of time to record it verbatim. A waste of your time. A waste of mine. The suggestion that Nayudu might be the murderer was a means of shocking him. A means of frightening him and softening him up. I think he suspected this . . . suspected it, but wasn't one hundred per cent sure.

Or, it may have been Chris's threat to expose him as an illegal immigrant.

Or, perhaps, the equally genuine threat to charge him with living off immoral earnings.

Whatever it was, he buckled; buckled as much as a man like Nayudu can *ever* buckle.

(In the event, the immoral earnings charge was never pressed. He provided what he was pleased to call 'insurance cover', and the contract, signed by every woman under his control, was too carefully worded to suggest that he knew their profession. It can be done. It often *is* done. The innocent-until-proven-guilty-beyond-reasonable-doubt clause is necessary but – as with men like Nayudu – it allows more than a few stinking fish room to swim through the meshes of its net.

The illegal immigrant charge? Nothing. Papers can be bought. Witnesses can be bribed. All it needs is money and friends in the right places. And Nayudu had both, in plenty.)

Chris was a good detective; a very practical detective. He guessed the probable final result of the interview and consequently was in a vile temper when he left Nayudu's house.

He flung himself behind the steering wheel, started the engine and said, 'Right, before we meet Lennox, let's have another look at the scene.'

'Will it do any good?' I asked.

'No. Nothing does any good,' he snarled. 'As policemen we're bloody useless. Worse than useless. You. Me. Every one of us. A slimy bastard like Nayudu – he's going to spit in our eye.'

'Hardly that.' I tried to mollify him. 'Hardly useless.'

'What else?'

In his anger he drove the car a little too fast.

'We do our best,' I murmured.

I knew what was wrong with him. He needed rest. He was becoming edgy; his nerves were starting to fray.

He'd been without sleep longer than I had. As a uniformed inspector, I'd followed the normal routine of night duty; the day before I'd had a few hours in bed. Not so, Chris. He'd worked through that day, then he'd been called out on the murder enquiry and had worked, non-stop, since then.

He was tired and tiredness can play havoc with a man's perspective. It can make wishful-thinking into near-certainty. Lack of sleep, lack of regular meals and too much concentrated effort; that's all that was wrong with Chris. Indeed he looked grey – almost ill – from lack of sleep.

He took a deep breath, then said, 'Eddie, you're too damn decent to be a copper. Y'know that? You lack the necessary hatred.'

'I don't like people like Nayudu,' I reminded him.

' "Like"?' His mouth moved into a slow, tight-lipped and twisted grin. A grin which was, in some strange way, savage and threatening. 'It isn't a matter of "liking". It isn't a matter of "disliking". It's a matter of hating. *Hating* the bastards. Hating their damn guts. Nayudu.

The animal who strangled the Walters woman. The scum we're paid to tame. It's that simple, Eddie. Hatred. The fuel that makes a police force function. Stop hating, the police machine grinds to a halt and crime isn't detected.'

It was quite a speech. I didn't agree with what he'd said. Come to that, *he* didn't believe what he'd said. It was tiredness and frustration talking. Tomorrow – after a good night's sleep – he'd know better. Objectivity, that's what he should have been talking about. Had he substituted the word 'objectivity' for the word 'hatred' he'd have been much nearer the truth.

But who can argue with a weary man? I allowed him to live with his temporary self-delusion.

We reached the scene of the crime.

Two uniformed constables and a uniformed sergeant stood guard at the entrance to the cul-de-sac. They looked bored. The enquiry had spread and was now well away from the place where the corpse had been found. But for the moment normal police procedure required a guard to remain at the scene.

One of the constables hurriedly nipped out a cigarette as he recognised us.

Not more than six non-police personnel were still at the scene. Newspapermen – the 'second team' – instructed to wait, in case the thousand-to-one chance of something interesting came along. If anything they looked even more bored than the policemen. A couple of them made a move towards us as we left the car, but Chris waved them aside.

'Wallace Yard,' I said as we walked into the dead-end street. 'It has to have a name. That's it. As you see, no houses. No offices. Just a few loading bays and the rear of some warehouses. That's Wallace's warehouse at the end. Presumably, that's where the name came from.'

'No street lighting,' observed Chris.

'No.' I smiled. 'There should be, but Bowling Side vandalism makes sure there never is.'

It was almost dark by this time and the cul-de-sac was a canyon of shadows. High-walled. Echoing slightly. We talked in low voices. It was not a place – not a time – which encouraged undue noise.

'There's something,' mused Chris.

'Something?'

'Something obvious. Something we've missed.'

'I don't see...'

'All lock-up property?'

'Yes. The warehouses. The loading bays. They're locked at night.'

'Usually?'

'Yes, usually.'

'But?'

'We find one open sometimes. The night-patrol constable checks. Usually twice each night. Sometimes he finds one open. Not a break-in. Not vandalism. Somebody forgets, that's all.'

'And?'

'The usual procedure. We have a list of key-holders. We pull one out of bed. After that, he tends to remember.'

'The man we're after.' Chris's voice was little more than a whisper. 'For the sake of argument, if he's a key-holder?'

I caught his train of thought and said, 'It is not impossible.'

'Bring her here,' murmured Chris. 'Murder her.'

'He could,' I agreed slowly, 'disappear from the face of the earth.'

'In at the back door. Out at the front . . . when the initial panic's died down. Easy.'

'Possible,' I agreed.

'Anybody check these doors?'

'No.' I corrected myself. 'I don't *think* so. Constable Turnbull didn't . . . we found the body before he tried any of the locks.'

'A point to remember.'

I agreed that it was a point to remember.

'Time of death?' mused Chris.

'We don't know. We'll know when we report in.'

'But not long. Right?'

'It's guessing,' I insisted.

'Dammit, she hadn't been dead long when you found her.'

'How long's "not long"?' I countered.

'Minutes.'

'For Heaven's sake, Chris!' I protested. 'Minutes. Yes . . . minutes. But how many minutes? Sixty. More than sixty? I don't know. The medical examination should be able to come up with something more specific.'

'You've handled corpses?'

'That doesn't make me an expert.'

'But you've handled 'em?'

'Of course.'

'And this one?'

'She was dead,' I sighed 'I touched the pulse point at the throat. She was still warm. That's as close as I'm prepared to commit myself.'

'Let's say minutes,' insisted Chris.

I hesitated, then said, 'All right, minutes.'

'Five minutes. Ten minutes.'

'I'm not prepared to . . .'

'For the sake of argument.'

Once more I hesitated, then I nodded and said, 'Just for the sake of argument.'

'No running footsteps,' said Chris.

'I'm sorry. I don't . . .'

'You came down Elvin Street?'

'Yes.' I nodded.

'You and Turnbull?'

'Yes.'

'It's one o'clock in the morning. Quiet. Dammit, it's quiet *now*. It must be like the grave in the small hours.'

'It is,' I agreed.

'You'd have heard.'

'Oh, for Heaven's sake!'

'Eddie, you'd have *heard* him. This place. It's like a sounding-board. You'd have . . .'

'No,' I cut in.

'What?'

'It won't do, Chris.'

'Meaning you *wouldn't* have heard? I'm damned if I see . . .'

'Meaning,' I said patiently, 'we don't yet know the time of death. Not even the approximate time. We can't build theories without that information. We can't! We can't even build decent possibilities. Somebody with a key – somebody who killed her then let himself into one of the warehouses. Somebody *without* a key – somebody who killed her then ran away. I didn't hear anybody. Constable Turnbull might have heard somebody – he was in this area long before I arrived – we'll ask him. Until we do? Chris . . . come down from Cloud Nine.'

Chris shook his head slowly. He took a few deep breaths, then smiled before he said, 'Good old Eddie. The voice of reason. I think it's time we reported to Lennox.'

The Recreation Room had undergone a transformation. It was now the complete Incident Centre. I think Lennox must have stayed there all day; only a man with his rank could have performed so much in so short a time. Typewriters and typists. Filing cabinets and filing clerks. In trays, Out trays, Pending trays and Urgent trays. Tables, chairs, blackboards, notice boards, large-scale maps of Bowling Side, three extra telephones, carefully worked-out rotas of officers and the streets they had to cover. It was all there. The complete Murder Enquiry launch pad. Lennox sat at a trestle table in one corner of the room; a gross queen bee controlling the buzz of workers feeding the honey of incoming data around the hive.

We found a couple of spare chairs, pulled them up to the table and began our report of the day's enquiries.

I allowed Chris to do the talking and, as each point was touched upon, Lennox nodded his head ponderously.

Then he rumbled, 'A couple of things about the corpse. Time of death between twelve-thirty and one. She was syphilitic. She was about two months' pregnant.'

Chris pursed his lips in a silent whistle.

'Aye.' Once more Lennox nodded. 'Two neat little motives, son.'

'Assuming the murderer knew,' I remarked.

'True,' agreed Lennox. 'These ladies don't warn customers about such things.'

'Manual strangulation?' said Chris. 'We've been working on that basis.'

'And savage,' added Lennox. 'The boy has muscles. Nothing under her fingernails and he stood in front of her. So she knew him, at a guess. She wasn't expecting it. And she hadn't time to do much in the way of retaliation. Nasty.'

'We've unearthed a name,' I reminded Lennox. 'Alfred . . .'

'Alfred Stone.' Lennox grinned; the grin of a conjuror producing a white rabbit. 'One of her street sisters saw 'em in Henry's café. A lad for the ladies . . . those sort o' ladies.'

'Has he been seen?' asked Chris.

'No.' The grin broadened. 'I thought you two might

40

fancy a go. He's under surveillance. Leave him till tomorrow. If it's him he'll be sweating. Pull him in tomorrow, eh? Play cat-and-mouse a little. He might crack.'

'With murder?' I murmured.

'Especially with murder.' Lennox's expression changed. He looked sombre. 'Caan, old son. Everybody has a conscience. They say they haven't, don't believe 'em. Scare the pants off 'em. Then watch the old conscience start working. For us. Not for them.'

'He'll crack,' growled Chris. 'If he's our man, he'll crack.'

I didn't agree, but nobody argues with a detective chief superintendent. Nor is it a nice thing to contradict a friend in the presence of a detective chief superintendent. I remained silent. Tomorrow, I thought, might be an interesting day; a hard interview with the man, Alfred Stone, could well prove them both wrong.

We mentioned the lock-up property which constituted Wallace Yard. We were too late. All the key-holders had been seen; all the key-holders had been carefully questioned; all the key-holders could account for their whereabouts. Lennox handed us a list of women's names and addresses.

'Street-walkers?' asked Chris.

'Some of 'em.' Lennox nodded. 'We've interviewed more slags than *that*. Those I've put ticks against. Friends – acquaintances – of the dead woman. We're getting 'em all cross-referenced. I'll leave those to you.'

'Bags of paperwork,' smiled Chris.

'These.' Lennox pulled a bundle of police photographs nearer. He chose one showing a close-up of the murder scene; a glossy black-and-white flash-bulb exposure, stark and uncompromising in its recording of every macabre feature.

41

'Observations?' he invited.

We examined the photograph.

'I've seen worse,' said Chris. 'It's not pleasant, but it's blood that makes 'em really nasty.'

'A good photograph,' I added. 'Get that to a jury and they'll know exactly what the trial's about.'

'The shoe.' Lennox took the photo from Chris, scowled at it, then continued, 'Think about it. You, Tallboy, you called 'em street-walkers. I know what you meant, but that's what they *are*. Literally. They pound the pavements. Like the rest of us they don't like sore feet. All right, they wear fancy shoes, but they wear fancy shoes that *fit*. One came adrift. How? Why?'

'In the struggle,' I said. 'Surely it's not significant . . .'

'It's significant that the other shoe didn't. That her hat's still in position, more or less. That there's no other *sign* of a struggle. A good strangler can do that, son. Quick. No mess. No noise. No struggle to mean anything. But a good fitting shoe comes off. And even the tights aren't laddered.'

'With respect . . .' began Chris.

'Say it, old son.' Lennox dropped the photograph back on top of the others. 'Forget rank. We're both chasing the same truth.'

'As Eddie says, where's the significance? The *real* significance? She lost her shoe. She lost her bloody *life*!'

'Constable Turnbull says he saw the shoe,' droned Lennox. 'He says if he hadn't spotted the shoe, the chances are he wouldn't have found the body.' Lennox glanced up at me. 'That right, Inspector?'

'I – er – I suppose so. I suppose it's possible.'

'The body was in a dark corner. In the entrance to a loading bay.'

'Yes,' I agreed.

'At least a yard from the shoe.'

'About that.'

'Who was using the torch?' asked Lennox.

'Turnbull, sir. On and off, the usual manner. To save the battery.'

'And Turnbull spotted the shoe?'

'I – er – I think we both saw it. At the same time.'

'And from the shoe, the body?'

I nodded.

'Without the shoe, no body?' said Lennox carefully.

'Well . . .' I hesitated then said, 'Eventually . . .'

'Ah, yes. *Eventually.*'

'It's hard to say. Impossible to say.'

'Is it important?' asked Chris brusquely.

'I dunno.' Lennox's moon-shaped face split into its grin. 'Who does know, old son? But – on the other hand – is anything *un*important on a murder enquiry.'

I drove Chris home and arranged to pick him up next morning. It seemed the kindest thing to do; he'd been driving most of the day and he was dog-tired.

He grumbled much of the way, a sure sign of weariness.

He said, 'That man!' Meaning Lennox. 'His marbles aren't all there. I swear they aren't. A complete song-and-dance routine about a damn shoe. So her shoe fell off? Jesus Christ, is that so important?'

'Lennox thinks so,' I murmured.

'How the hell he got to be a chief superintendent . . .'

'He's no mug, Chris,' I warned him gently. 'Too many people have been conned by that ho-ho-ho-Father-Christmas exterior.'

Chris refused to be pacified; he remained tetchy and, as I dropped him at his gate, I refused an invitation of a quick drink and suggested that he get to bed and enjoy as much sleep as possible.

As for myself, I couldn't sleep until well past midnight.

The shoe episode worried me. Lennox had a reputation for making everything fit. Everything! The shoe which apparently *shouldn't* have fallen off, was no longer a 'nothing'. It was no longer unimportant. Indeed it was very important, if only because Detective Chief Superintendent Lennox was seeking a reason.

But I slept at last and was up and having a quick breakfast before eight. I called for Chris, drove him to Bowling Side Police Station and together we checked on what little the night's enquiries had to offer. The names of a few more whores. Nothing else.

'Okay.' Chris stretched the aftermath of tiredness from his arms and shoulders. 'Alfred Stone, I think.'

'Self-employed. Small-time builder.' I consulted a flimsy which one of the telephonists had handed to me. 'According to the tail we have on him he's just arrived at a bungalow, *Reach-Me-Down*, – on the outskirts of Kemington.'

'What bloody names people come up with for their houses.'

'Bungalows,' I smiled.

'Okay, Kemington here we come.'

Once more I drove. The bungalow wasn't hard to find; with a name like that how could it be? We braked at the gate leading to a flower-bordered path and, beyond the gate, we could see three men busy erecting an extension porch to the side door. Two of the men were working under the direction of the third. The third man – Alfred Stone, obviously.

He was a short man. Thick-built. With close-cropped, curly hair. A very muscular man and, from the manner in which he gave instructions to his companions, a very self-confident man. Age? At a guess between thirty-five and forty. Possibly just a little older. He was wearing an old jacket over bibbed overalls. His concentration upon

44

what he was doing was such that he was unaware of our presence until Chris spoke.

'Alfred Stone?'

'Eh?' He turned his head without moving his body.

I watched the man's hands. Big hands with thick, spatulate fingers. Strong hands with an excess of hair on their backs. Hands which could strangle very easily. I glanced at Chris. Chris, too, had noticed the hands.

'Alfred Stone?' repeated Chris.

'Who wants to know?'

'Police.' Chris slipped his warrant card from his breast pocket and held it for Stone to see. He said, 'We'd like words.'

'Can't you see I'm busy?' Stone scowled.

'So are we. This isn't a social call.'

'Can't it wait?' grumbled Stone.

'No.' Chris's voice was flat and conclusive.

Stone hesitated. For a moment I thought he was going to give us trouble. Then he nodded, surlily, gave his two staring colleagues terse instructions and followed us to the waiting car. Chris sat in the back with Stone. I drove.

After about five minutes of silence Stone said, 'Aren't I allowed to know then?'

'We think you might know without being told,' said Chris grimly.

'I don't see how the hell . . .'

'If you don't know, we'll tell you.'

'When?'

'In good time.'

I could hear Stone's deep breath before he said, 'What about a solicitor?'

Chris said, 'If we pass one, wave.'

Nothing more was said until we reached Kemington D.H.Q.

In the D.H.Q. building Chris handed Stone over to a

uniformed constable and said, 'Number Three Interview Room. Sit with him. Ears open, mouth shut. We'll be along in a few minutes.'

'Yes, sir.' The constable led Stone away.

We climbed the steps to the C.I.D. Office and from there Chris telephoned Headquarters and, from Criminal Records and Intelligence, got what information they could provide about Stone.

Then we joined Stone in Number Three Interview Room and dismissed the constable.

Interview rooms. Odd. Even when you're on the right side – even when *you're* the one asking the questions – they have a strange, intimidatory atmosphere. There must be a reason. The proportions, perhaps; they are never small enough to be called closets, but they are rarely large enough to merit the name 'room'; it is as if some skilled architect has come up with the ideal claustrophobic proportions. Nothing can be said that cannot be heard. No movement can be made that cannot be seen. They are the epitome of non-privacy.

Their furniture rarely varies. A simple, polished table; usually with a drawer in which are kept statement forms, handy for when they are required. Two chairs; never more than three. Chairs in which one may sit, but in which one may not relax. Chairs of the 'kitchen' variety or (as in the case of Number Three Interview Room) of the canvas and tubular-steel variety. (In this case there were three chairs.) An ashtray. Cheap, tin and clean of any marks of ash; a silent invitation to a cigarette smoker, an invitation which he may accept subject to certain provisos.

Rubber hoses, strong lights, all the paraphernalia of the infamous third-degree interrogation are unnecessary in a purpose-built, properly furnished, interview room. The room itself is enough. The room itself gradually creates a condition in which gentle terror becomes an accepted part of normality.

We each sat in a chair. Chris conducted the interview, with very rare moments in which I introduced an odd question or two. Chris never raised his voice above an occasional sharply spoken reprimand. Stone began, as most of them do, by blustering.

'Look! I want to know what right . . .'

'A murder enquiry carries almost limitless rights, Stone.'

'*A murder enquiry?*'

'You don't think you're here to buy tickets for the Police Dance, do you?'

'What the hell do I know about . . .'

'You'll tell us what you know. Eventually.'

'Look. I want a lawyer.'

'Why?'

'I've the bloody right . . .'

'Why do you need a lawyer, Stone?'

'For Christ's sake! You've just . . .'

'What?'

'Eh?'

'I've just what?'

'You – you . . .'

'Do you want to make a confession? Already?'

'What the . . . What the *hell* . . .'

'I could ask the same question. What the hell do you want with a lawyer?'

'I – I dunno. It's just that – that . . .'

'That you're scared.'

'What the hell have I to be scared about?'

'You tell us.'

'Look, mister . . .'

'Inspector. Inspector Tallboy.'

'All right – Inspector Tallboy – I don't know what the

hell all this is about. Tell me, okay? Tell me. Then if I can, I'll help.'

'No lawyers?'

'If – if I need a lawyer, I'll say. Right?'

'Murder,' said Chris gently.

'Eh?'

'You read newspapers?'

'The sports pages. That's all. All the rest is . . .'

'You watch television?'

'No. It's so much crap.'

'Don't you ever *talk* to anybody?'

'What the Christ Almighty are these questions about? Newspapers? Television? Talking to people? What the bloody hell . . .'

'It's top news locally.'

'What is?'

'Murder. The murder of Emilia Walters.'

'Who?'

'Emilia Walters. She was strangled, the night before last.'

'So, what the hell . . .'

'In Bowling Side.'

'Oh!'

It was like a punctuation mark in the interview; a deliberate pause, as Stone opened his eyes a little wider, lost much of his bluster and began to look slightly apprehensive.

'You were there,' said Chris, quietly.

'Where?'

'Bowling Side.'

'Who says I was . . .'

'You're not the invisible man. People know you. You were there.'

'All right. But I wasn't the only . . .'

'At the time of the murder.'

'Eh?'

'You were in Bowling Side, at the time of the murder.'

'I dunno what time the . . .'

'When you were there. When you were in Bowling Side. *That's* when the murder was committed.'

'Bloody hell! Is that all . . .'

'With the dead woman.'

'Where the hell d'you get *that*. I don't even know anybody called . . .'

'Samantha?'

'W-what?'

'That was her – er . . . stage name. Emilia Walters.'

'Samantha?'

All the bluster had gone now. Only apprehension remained and the apprehension was gradually melting into panic.

'Suppose we start from there,' suggested Chris. 'Bowling Side. Samantha. You being with her. Her being strangled. Let's start there.'

It was a sordid, pathetic story. A disjointed story, told in spurts and liberally laced with mild bad language. We 'knew how it was', being men of the world. A 'bit of variety', that's why he visited Bowling Side. He knew quite a few of the women. He named them. He knew Samantha – quite liked Samantha, she 'gave good value for money'. He'd been with her. 'Y'know – been with her.' Then they'd visited Henry's place. A bit of an argument; not much, just a bit of an argument. Then he'd left her and returned home. About midnight, he thought. He wasn't sure. He hadn't checked the time – who the hell keeps looking at his watch? – but about midnight.

'The argument?' asked Chris.

'Not much.' Stone was genuinely frightened by this time. 'Just – y'know – a difference of opinion.'

'About what?'

'Politics.'

Chris stared, disbelievingly.

'Politics?' I spoke for the first time.

'Labour. Tory. Y'know, *politics.*'

'With a whore?' I, too, was finding it hard to believe. Stone said, 'They have a bloody vote, y'know. They have opinions.'

'I – er – yes, I suppose they do.'

'Silly cow was Labour.' He sounded almost aggrieved.

'You're not?' I murmured.

'Bloody likely! I've enough on without having the sodding unions breathing down the back of my neck. I'm Tory, see? Free enterprise. To hell with helping all the lazy buggers. Let 'em starve. It's their own bleeding . . .'

'You left her at – or about – midnight?' chimed in Chris.

'Near enough.'

'Went home?'

Stone nodded.

'Walk?'

'No. At that time of night? It's a long way. I took a taxi.'

'There'll be a record then?'

'What?'

'The taxi – what time it picked you up.'

'I – er – I went to the office. Y'know . . . the office.'

'Which firm?'

'Kemington Hire.'

'Shall I . . .' I began.

'Later.' Chris kept his eyes on Stone's face. 'Pass anybody?' he asked.

'Eh?'

'Did you pass anybody? Speak to anybody? After you'd left the Walters woman?'

'No. I dunno. Who the hell . . .' He stopped, slapped

50

his thigh, then said, 'Yes by Christ. The bloody copper.'

'A policeman?' I said. 'You passed a policeman?'

Stone nodded.

Chris said, 'He'd notice you, you think?'

'The daft bugger stopped me.'

'Stopped you?' Interest crept into Chris's tone.

'Asked me who I was. What I was doing out at that time.'

'You told him?'

'I told him who I was. I told him I was going home after a business appointment. You don't tell a bobby . . .'

'Did you get his number?' I asked.

'His number?'

'On his shoulder,' said Chris. 'Chrome-plated numbers on the shoulders of his uniform. Did you get them?'

'No.'

'Describe him,' said Chris.

'I dunno. They all look the same. How can you . . .'

'Try.'

Stone tried. He tried very hard. It was a poor description; it *could* have fitted Constable Turnbull: it could have fitted almost half the constables on patrol that night.

'We'll check.' Chris seemed to relax a little. He said, 'A point of interest, Stone. Why do you do it?'

'What?'

'Go with prostitutes? You're a married man. Four kids. Why prostitutes?'

'It makes a change,' he muttered.

'That's a lousy excuse.'

'Think so?' Bitterness – perhaps bitterness, perhaps contempt – touched Stone's voice. 'My old woman. In the club every bloody time. Four kids, see? Four kids, and we've lost two before they were born. Stuff that for a lark. She catches a draught from my shirt-tail and she's up the spout again. Stuff *that*, eh?'

51

'The pill's been invented,' Chris reminded him.

'She doesn't believe in 'em. Bad for the heart, that's what she's read somewhere. Jesus wept! What about *my* heart? What about my bloody pocket? Kids don't live on fresh air.'

'So, you go with prostitutes?'

'Prozzies take precautions.'

'This one didn't,' said Chris teasingly.

'Eh?'

'Virility, Stone. That's your complaint. You can even give prostitutes kids.'

'Me?'

'Somebody.'

'The hell, it can't be me. You can't prove it was *me*.'

'Let's assume it was,' suggested Chris.

'I'm telling you. It...'

'Just an assumption. For the sake of argument.'

'What argument?'

'It would,' said Chris pointedly, 'be a neat motive for murder.'

'I've already told you, I didn't...'

'People tell us so many things.' Chris smiled.

'Look, I've told you, the copper...'

'He'll be seen.' Chris paused, then added, 'Meanwhile take my tip. Be careful where you put your chopper.'

'Eh?' Stone stared.

'She wasn't only pregnant,' said Chris bluntly, 'she was also poxed up to the eyeballs.'

'Holy cow!' Instinctively, it seemed, one of Stone's hands flew to his crotch.

'An occupational hazard.' Chris's smile was cold and sardonic. 'And, of course, one more possible motive for murder.'

'I didn't! For Christ's sake... *I didn't kill the dirty bitch.*'

52

Chris murmured, 'So you say. So they *all* say . . . at first.'

And from that moment Stone was a terrified man.

The interview continued for more than two hours. A beautifully paced interview; beautiful, that is, if viewed objectively and as an exercise in the forcing of sweat from the pores of a man being tortured on the rack of interrogation. Chris was an artist. Not for him the blunt instrument of out-and-out disbelief; to call a suspect a liar every time he opens his mouth – every time he answers a question – is to bludgeon him into a state of moral and mental punch-drunkenness. But if, like Chris, you merely express *doubt*, then watch him wriggle and twist and turn in a thousand attempts to convince. Instead of sullen silence there is a surfeit of talk. Gentle sarcasm. Sardonic amusement. The mildly contemptuous smile. These are the weapons of the born inquisitor. These were the weapons used on Stone by Chris.

I said little. But I watched. I watched the face of a hard man crumple into a child's mask of alarm. I heard a voice which was once harsh and demanding turn into a trembling whisper of desperation. And I watched the hands – those broad hands with those muscular fingers, those hands which could so easily squeeze the life from a fellow-being – twist and tie themselves into knots, as Chris eased the knife-edge of each question a hair's-breadth deeper.

An opinion, for what it's worth, had he been the strangler, I think Stone would have broken under that questioning.

We had a belated lunch at a restaurant not far from Kemington D.H.Q. Sausage and mash followed by apple pie and custard and ending with coffee, cheese and biscuits. Filling, but not flamboyant. The sort of

53

meal we both needed after the prolonged session with Stone; something to bring us out of the sombre, Giant Land of a hard murder enquiry and, for the moment at least, return us to near-normality.

And yet the conversation as we smoked our after-meal cigarettes turned to the possibility of Stone being the man responsible for the Walters woman's killing.

'Turnbull could clear him,' I suggested.

'Turnbull could put him right there, where the murder was committed,' contradicted Chris.

'Oh!' Each coin, it would seem, had two sides.

'The taxi people *might* clear him,' conceded Chris.

'Might?'

'These homicidal idiots.' Chris sighed drew on his cigarette and as he exhaled smoke, continued. 'They think up some fancy alibi. Always. A taxi from the scene, which we're invited to check. Then another taxi *back* to the scene, which we aren't expected to even *suspect*.'

'You have,' I smiled, 'a tortuous mind.'

'Like flat feet, it goes with the job.'

For the rest of that day we interviewed whores and friends of whores. Some were openly antagonistic; to them we were 'the enemy' and that one of their number had been murdered left them unmoved. A natural reaction? Yes, I suppose so. Lewdness, immorality, fiscal fornication, that coupled with the present permissive society, doesn't fit too snugly into law enforcement; it can't be eradicated because it's too much a part of so-called civilisation, it's been with us since the dawn of history, therefore it isn't some new gimmick which can be destroyed by being discouraged and then allowed to run its course. It can only be hounded by various forms of 'vice squad', *ergo* a percentage (a large percentage) of those who live from it look upon all policemen as their antagonists.

54

Some few – the younger, less blatantly disgusting types – were shocked at the murder of one of their sisters. Some knew her. Some didn't. But, I think, they all appreciated that *they* might quite easily have been the victim. This, as I say, from a few, but the majority refused to acknowledge even this possibility.

That evening we reported to Lennox and in turn were brought up to date on the enquiry. Between seventy and eighty officers had been detailed for full-time investigation; the majority of them were engaged on standard house-to-house visits: men sifting through the haystack of non-information in the blind hope that one of them might prick his finger on the needle of solid fact. Two more pairs, like Chris and myself, had been given 'roving commissions' in the equally pious hope that experience and gut policing might short-cut the dreary question-and-answer routine. The press and local TV News had been fed their required platitudes. Already a number of pathetic creatures had 'confessed' to the crime; men (and one woman) to whom possibly notoriety seemed the only means of escaping from a life whose boredom had driven them to the brink of insanity. It was a murder enquiry, with all the usual spin-offs.

'The father's coming up to identify the body, first thing tomorrow morning,' said Lennox. 'Reading – the family took some tracing. He'll stay over for the inquest.'

'You want us there?' asked Chris.

'Aye.' Lennox wobbled his chins in a nod. 'Meet him at the station. 9.54. She's at Kemington Royal Infirmary. Take him for a meal, inquest at two o'clock.' He paused, then added, 'He might be able to help. A decent family by the sound o' things. Daughters don't go on the bash without some sort o' reason. It might help.'

'We'll try,' promised Chris.

'Meanwhile catch up with some sleep. I'll get Stone's

55

story either verified or the other thing. The results'll be waiting for you tomorrow. Take it from there.' He gave a ponderous sigh and ended, 'I have this feeling we're in for a long slog.'

That night I read aloud to Mother. She sat in bed, propped up by pillows and with a knitted wool jacket across her shoulders. Downstairs Aunt Elizabeth busied herself tidying the loose ends of the day and occasionally we heard a door close or the rattle of crockery as she washed the cups we'd used for our late evening drink.

I read, '*I could not, in those days, see God for this creature: of whom I had made an idol.*'

I closed the book as I ended chapter twenty-four and smiled at Mother.

'As beautiful as ever,' she remarked.

'I think so,' I agreed.

'Why so few of us these days?' she mused. Her voice was tinged with sadness.

'We live in a foul world. Charlotte Brontë would never have understood. *Jane Eyre* could never have been written.'

'I wonder.'

'I *know*,' I insisted.

'I sometimes regret . . .' She stopped as if unwilling to complete the sentence.

'What?'

'You like your job?' she asked.

'Of course.' The question surprised me. I added, 'Most of the time.'

'Christopher?' she asked gently.

'No, not Chris.' I frowned as I tried to collect my thoughts. 'Chris is an excellent policeman. And my friend.'

'But coarse?' she suggested.

'A gentleman by comparison.' I half-smiled. 'Some of my colleagues really would shock you, and not deliberately.'

'You dislike it?'

'I uphold the law, Mother.' I spoke slowly and chose my words with care. 'The law – as I see it – is the basic, common denominator upon which morals can be built. We don't concern ourselves with morals. They are beyond our terms of reference. But if we enforce the law, then there is a base.'

'And these creatures you are expected to visit? To question?'

'That I don't enjoy,' I admitted.

'Because they disgust you?'

'Yes,' I admitted. 'They disgust me. But I also feel sorry for them.'

'They have a choice.'

'They have a choice,' I agreed. 'But they lack the courage to make a choice.'

'Unless . . .' She paused and watched me.

'Mother.' I stood up from my chair. 'I've had a hard day. I have a headache. I think a short stroll, a little fresh air, then bed.'

'Good night, Edmund.' She held up her cheek to be kissed.

I said, 'Good night, Mother,' kissed her, then left the bedroom.

It was raining outside; a cool, September drizzle which gave every street lamp its own rainbow-coloured halo. It moistened my face and cleared the vague, nagging ache at the nape of my neck. It seemed to cleanse my mind, washing away those half-doubts and near-worries which always seemed to accompany any prolonged conversation with Mother.

Aunt Elizabeth had retired when I got back so I let myself in, bathed, changed into pyjamas and dressing-gown and enjoyed a quiet, last-cigarette-of-the-day before I went to bed.

I was more tired than I thought. In no time at all I was asleep. I dreamed. Vivid, but not unpleasant dreams. In them Sarah was still a child. Still . . .

THREE

Where was I?

Ah, yes, I slept well. Nevertheless, it was still dark when the telephone bell awakened me. I climbed from bed and before going down to the hall I glanced at my watch. It was just after 4 a.m.

Chris's voice came over the wire. Agitated. Almost excited.

'Get yourself down here, Eddie. There's another one.'

'Another what?'

'Another killing. Another strangling.'

Aunt Elizabeth appeared on the landing and called, 'What is it, Eddie? Who's calling?'

'It's all right, Aunt Elizabeth. It's – it's police work.'

Chris's voice said, 'Another prozzy. Carlotta, this time.'

'Chris.' I waved Aunt Elizabeth silent and concentrated upon what I was being told. I said, 'Where are you?'

'Bowling Side nick. Get down here, fast. Lennox is on his way. All hell's breaking.'

'I'll be there.'

I dropped the receiver on to its rest, ran up the stairs, elbowed my way past Aunt Elizabeth, slammed the door of my room and began to dress.

'Two in three days.' Harris made the remark sound like an accusation. He was justified, I suppose. From where he stood what else but an accusation? What else but sloppy police work? He stared at Lennox and said, 'It looks bad, Chief Superintendent.'

Lennox bobbed his head.

At four-fifteen on a wet, September morning the world

59

is rarely a happy place. It is made less happy when an assistant chief constable has been dragged from his bed. It is made positively miserable when, as one of a group, you stand at the rear of a filthy café and, for the second time in three nights, await the arrival of photographers and all the rest of them, whom police procedure insists must dance attendance upon a dead whore.

For want of something to say, I asked, 'Where is she?'

'Behind the dustbins.' Chris moved his head. 'The coat – see it? – draped over one of the bins, that's why they found her. They saw the coat first.'

'They?'

'Sergeant Hobson . . . and P.C. Turnbull.'

'Turnbull!' We spoke in little more than whispers in order not to impinge our presence upon Harris, Lennox, Warlock and Perkins. I said, 'He's making a habit of . . .'

Chris touched my arm and we moved a few yards from the group.

'He's in a hell of a state,' said Chris.

'Turnbull?'

'Wouldn't you be?'

'Where is he?' I asked.

'In the café with Hobson.' Chris glanced at the group of senior officers, then added, 'C'mon. He needs a bit of moral support.'

I didn't like the idea too much, but I didn't protest. We walked away from the quartet of rank, skirted the side of the café, kept well clear of the growing numbers of policemen and civilians and slipped in through the front door. The uniformed constable standing guard made no attempt to bar our entrance; presumably he took it for granted that a detective inspector, and the inspector in charge of the section, had automatic right of entry.

The place was as disgusting, as stinking, as ever. Cats

galore. The same haze of stale cigarette smoke. Henry unshaven and padding around in his stocking-feet. And Turnbull and Sergeant Hobson.

Turnbull was sitting at one of the tables. Helmet off, forearms resting on the table-top and, held in both hands, a mug from which he sipped occasionally. In some strange way he looked broken, physically broken; as if his spine, or some major bone in his body, had snapped.

Hobson was seated alongside him with an arm across the younger man's shoulders. Paternal. Comforting. Murmuring what must have been words of encouragement into the constable's ear. Hobson saw us enter, but made no move to stand up.

We walked to the table and Chris said, '*Somebody* had to find her, Turnbull.'

Turnbull didn't seem to hear. He sipped at the liquid in the cup and pulled a wry face.

'What's he drinking?' I asked the question of Henry.

'Rum.'

'He needs brandy. Whisky.'

'I only keep rum,' said Henry. 'I like a tot, before I go to bed.'

'It's – it's all right, sir.' Turnbull raised his head long enough to look at me as he spoke.

'Who sent you in here?' asked Chris.

'Mr Lennox.'

'Me with him, sir.' Hobson sent messages with his eyes. 'To see he was okay.'

'Second time round?' Questions had to be asked and answered. I asked the question as gently as I could.

'Sir?' Turnbull took a deep, shuddering breath then tried to pull himself together. He looked up at me as he spoke.

I said, 'Property checking. Second time round?'

'Yes, sir. I've told Mr Lennox . . .'

'Tell me.'

'Second check of the night, sir. I checked this place at about midnight, maybe a bit after. She – she wasn't there then.'

'You're sure?'

'The coat – the coat . . .'

'The coat wasn't there?'

'No, sir. The coat wasn't there.'

'But the body?'

'I didn't look. The dustbins, I didn't look behind the dustbins.'

'This place,' said Chris. 'Was it still open the first time you checked.'

'Yes, sir. It was still open. I glanced in. A handful of customers.'

'We closed about one,' contributed Henry.

Hobson frowned his worry. Chris remained stone-faced. I think we all knew. The question : why check property not yet locked up? What point was there in checking the rear door of a café which was still open? I knew, Hobson knew, and Chris had seen the area closely enough to guess. This part of Bowling Side – between the canal and Lessfield Road – was a mass of lock-up property. Scores, hundreds, of premises to be checked. To do the job properly – to check them twice a night – was possible, but only just. If anything interfered with the door-checking, the twice-nightly visit became impossible and much of the property was visited only once.

'Anything last night other than the murder?' I asked.

'Nothing,' said Hobson quietly. He guessed my line of thought and added, 'Turnbull, here, wirelessed it in at three-eighteen. It's logged.'

I nodded.

Turnbull looked up at me with hurt eyes and muttered, 'You – you think . . .'

'Nothing,' I interrupted gently. 'You found the body. That's all.'

'I found the other body.'

'*We* found the other body,' I corrected him.

'It's your beat,' said Chris. 'Murder victims . . . who else should find them?' He turned to Henry and said, 'You. The last time you went outside? The last time you used the rear door?'

'I – I dunno.'

'You'd better bloody know.'

'Look, I don't keep time sheets. I can't remember . . .'

'Remember,' snapped Chris.

'Two tarts.' I added my weight to that of Chris. 'They both use this place. You know them. They're both murdered. One of them is murdered on your back door-step. As Inspector Tallboy says, you'd *better* know a few things.'

Turnbull muttered, 'She was in here.'

'You're sure?' Hobson asked the question.

'When I looked in. Carlotta was one of the customers.'

'Well?' Chris aimed the word at Henry and lifted one eyebrow fractionally. 'Was she?'

'W-what?'

'Here? In this dump?'

'Sure. Sure she was here. That doesn't mean . . .'

'It means,' said Chris, 'you could be the last person to have seen her alive.'

'Or,' I added, 'the first person to have seen her dead.'

It was a deliberate ploy of course. Consider, would a man having killed a whore dump that whore on his own back doorstep? No, of course not. Not, that is unless he was trying for a double bluff. And Henry lacked the intelligence to attempt *that*. Henry was a simple-minded lout and, to a large extent, his very simple-mindedness pre-

63

cluded him from serious suspicion. He would in time be 'leaned upon'. He would be *made* to remember; made to remember things which, at that moment, he was prepared to swear he'd forgotten.

But for the moment . . .

The ploy was for Turnbull's benefit. It was meant to demonstrate that people, other than himself, could be under suspicion. His guilt – his innocence – didn't come into it. His mental state *did*. Guilty, he'd crack. But innocent, he had at least to be in a state of mind capable of fighting back. Henry? Who the hell was Henry? Who cared about a fiddling little eating-house owner who catered for scum? Henry was a means to an end, and we used him.

It was, I suppose, a 'closing of ranks', but if so what of it? Turnbull needed a crutch. Chris was fashioning that crutch and I saw no reason to destroy the crutch before Turnbull could test it for strength.

Harris stayed at the scene; for the moment he took over the on-the-spot responsibility of gingering up the initial enquiries, of giving stock answers to the stock questions asked by members of the media, of quietening down the growing panic of the Bowling Siders. Perkins and Sergeant Hobson stayed with him.

The rest of us – Lennox, Warlock, Chris, Turnbull and myself – made our way back to Bowling Side Police Station and assembled in my office. It was something of a crush, but we needed privacy the Incident Centre couldn't provide.

Our immediate problem was Turnbull.

'It ain't easy.' Lennox filled the swivel-chair behind my desk. He crossed a palm across his bald pate, looked up at Turnbull and repeated, 'You realise that, old son? It ain't easy.'

'I – I realise that, sir.'

Turnbull had regained some control over himself. Too much control perhaps; he stood stiff muscled and expressionless, robot-like and with the voice of a robot.

Warlock said, 'Suspension from duty pending the result of enquiries. The obvious answer.'

'No.' Lennox shook his head.

'It seems to me . . .'

'It'll be in every bloody newspaper,' growled Lennox.

'Tried. Found guilty,' muttered Turnbull.

'And if you *are* guilty?' snapped Warlock.

'He'll get nailed.' Lennox answered the question. He made it a simple statement of fact. He added, 'But it'll be a trial. By a court of law, not by the press and television.'

'If he's allowed to continue on duty . . .'

'He won't be.' Lennox looked at the miserable Turnbull, gave a quick twisted grin, then said, 'Compassionate leave. That suit?'

'I – I . . .'

'And the reason?' asked Warlock.

'Personal reasons. He's told me in confidence.'

'Of all the . . .'

'Sir. May I have compassionate leave?' Turnbull spoke directly to Lennox.

'Why not, son?' The charade was played out between the two of them as if Warlock, Chris and I weren't there. 'Indefinite?'

'If that's possible, sir.'

'It's possible.' Lennox nodded. 'Make out the form, I'll sign it. Then away home.'

'Thank you, sir.'

Turnbull saluted, then turned to leave the office.

Before he reached the door, I said, 'Turnbull.'

'Sir?'

'Home . . . understand? If we need you we want to know where to find you.'

'I'll be at home, sir.'

Retrospect wisdom is, I suppose, the easiest and cheapest wisdom of all. Anybody can put the required two and two together, once they know the final four. And yet . . .

I think I knew. I think I sensed it before Turnbull left the office. Warlock was a dangerous man to cross, easily offended and capable of carrying spite to almost ridiculous lengths. And, the other side of the coin, Lennox was not the most tactful man in the world; he just didn't give a damn for protocol or other people's feelings. It boiled down to this : Lennox was a law unto himself, but Warlock was the law within Kemington Division.

Something had to break and – or so it seemed – Police Constable Turnbull was the most fragile object available.

As we drove out to Bowling Side I voiced my questions. 'Turnbull?' I suggested.

'He dislikes prostitutes.' Chris watched the road ahead and kept the car at a steady twenty-five.

'Turnbull?' It was still a question, but this time a surprised question.

'Or,' mused Chris, 'he dislikes – *disliked* – these two particular prostitutes.'

'Are you talking about Turnbull?'

'They lived together, that could be the link. Or maybe a clue to the link.'

'Chris, are you . . .'

'No, I'm not talking about Turnbull.' He braked slightly as a stray cat darted out of an alley and threatened to run into the path of the car.

I said, 'Warlock seems pretty sure . . .'

'Warlock is a mad bastard, and vindictive with it.'

'He could be right,' I suggested.

'He could be right,' agreed Chris. 'Equally he could be wrong. He's already made up his mind, and that makes him a damn fool.'

'He – er – he found both bodies,' I reminded him.

'Are you playing devil's advocate?'

'No. I'm reviewing what few facts we have to work on.'

'You found one body.' He turned his head for a moment, saw the look on my face, then laughed and added, 'Okay, now *I'm* playing devil's advocate. He found two. You found one. If he's guilty, you're half-guilty.'

'The hell I'm . . .'

'Look, Eddie.' He reduced speed even more as we entered the web of streets in which the murders had been committed. He said, 'You saw him in the café, in Henry's place. That wasn't acting, that was honest-to-God shock . . . and no man can act shock well enough to make it look like the real thing.'

I nodded agreement.

'But,' he continued, 'whoever did do the killing wanted the bodies found. The shoe . . . Lennox was wise enough to spot the shoe. Now the coat. That coat was there to make 'em look. *Them*, don't forget that little point. Turnbull and you. Now Turnbull and Hobson. Always somebody with him. Always something to attract the attention.'

'Always?' I smiled. 'Twice, that's a very poverty-stricken "always".'

'I have a gut feeling,' muttered Chris. And he *wasn't* smiling.

Kale Court. Bowling Side – especially the stretch between the canal and Lessford Road – has a few score 'Kale Courts'. They all have a name. They all have a different name. Vermin, too, I suppose. Scores, hundreds, of foul and stinking things come under the general umbrella of 'vermin'. They all have a name, but they're all vermin.

The same with Kale Court.

It stank, literally. Generations of beer-heavy drunks had used its walls as a handy, albeit unofficial, urinal. The not-too-fussy good-time girls had taken advantage of its darkened privacy for the colloquial 'quickie'. Used condoms, dog mess, blocked drains, rotting vegetable leaves, cat piss . . . you name it, that's what it smelled of.

It had been home to Emilia Walters (trade name 'Samantha') and Bertha Hewitt (trade name 'Carlotta'). It was still home for almost a dozen other whores. Every house was apportioned off into 'rooms'. Each set of 'rooms' housed at least one, more often two, women of the street.

'Jesus Christ!' Chris spoke for both of us. 'This is what the silly bitches call "glamour".'

'They know the score.' The woman climbed the stairs ahead of us and spoke without turning. 'And,' she added, 'a girl gets on her back because a guy pays her . . . right? It takes two to make a screw. Don't forget that.'

The philosophy of whoredom and this worn-out hag was reminding us of it. She owned the house; she rented the rooms. Last time we hadn't needed her. The Hewitt woman had been at home and had opened the door of the rooms to our knock. This time the Hewitt woman was dead and we needed the landlady and her pass-key.

She watched us as we opened drawers and cupboards. As we dragged cheap suitcases from under the beds. It was a good search. A thorough search. But all we found was cheap finery; paste jewellery; a well-thumbed book of pornographic photographs. We found letters and postcards; poor, pathetic communications sent by parents, aunts, sisters; unimportant snippets of news from a world of respectability.

'Any friends?' asked Chris.

'Lots of friends,' said the woman cynically. 'Pay the

68

asking price, you could have been her "friend" by the hour.'

'Don't get too bloody smart,' warned Chris. 'They're dead. Both of 'em.'

'Count the wreaths,' suggested the woman.

'I've already warned you not to be . . .'

'Shove it, mister!' The woman fought back, like a middle-aged wild-cat. Her eyes shone hatred and she spat the words, as she said, 'Animals – dogs, cats – *they* get more understanding than these kids. Ask around. Next door. A bloody parson's daughter. A *parson's* daughter. And the rest. They ain't all bad. Most . . . they're going to get it. They're going to get hurt or they're going to get paid, but either way they're going to get it. They take the easy way. You blame 'em? All that crap in the news-papers. Film stars. Creeps in pop groups. Money, mister, *money*! That's the reason. The only reason. They're not nympho. They're ordinary. But earning it on your back is respectable these days. Cows with their photographs in the newspapers every week. Why not these kids, eh? What's so damn different, once the clothes come off?

'And they're normal, right? Okay, they're normal. The pansies – the gay bastards – they're "understood". Eh? Shove it in the wrong hole, and everybody breaks a leg making excuses. These kids can't understand. Who the hell can?' She quietened suddenly, then softly and on the verge of tears, said, 'They're nice kids, mister. Nice kids. You live this life – see if you can stay as nice as they are.'

'They're slags,' I said flatly.

'Yeah, slags.' She hesitated, then said, 'So what does that make your man?'

'Come again?' Chris looked up from where he was flipping through a three-year-old diary.

'Forget it.'

'No.' Chris straightened. ' "Our man". Who the hell's "our man"?'

'You don't know?' Disbelief hung on the question.

'Tell me,' invited Chris. 'Let's assume I'm the only man on God's earth who doesn't know. Who is he? And what *should* I know?'

Turnbull, of course. To set a man in a garden of forbidden fruit and expect him not to weaken and taste is to ask much. It is to ask *too* much, if the man is weak. And Turnbull was a weak man. Obviously his break-up in the café in the early hours of that morning had proved that much.

My surprise was that *Chris* was surprised. Such naivety from a police officer – from a detective inspector – amazed me. He had (I've said it before) a code of ethics which was completely illogical. A code of ethics which blinded him to the obvious.

He drove me back to Bowling Side Police Station to pick up my car and I was amazed at the simplicity of the man.

'It happens, Chris,' I said patiently.

'Are you trying to exonerate it?' His voice was harsh with disillusionment.

'Not exonerate. Explain.'

'Moral blackmail,' he snarled. 'The poor bitches . . .'

'The harlots,' I reminded him. 'The trollops. The woman was biased. Don't let her cloud your judgement.'

'What she said was true. They're . . .'

'What she said,' I interrupted, 'was balls. They became whores because they *want* to become whores. That's the only reason. Everything else is an excuse. Lust. Carnality. Fornication. Perversion. Good God, Chris! They're not innocents. They aren't now, they weren't at the beginning.

Harlotry is a profession. A chosen profession. They made a choice.'

'Policing's a profession, too,' growled Chris.

'True,' I agreed.

'And Turnbull's a damn...'

'Turnbull is a fornicator. That in itself takes him no nearer to being a murderer.'

'It does, by God.'

'In that case, we'll do well to remember Stone.'

'I'm sorry.' He frowned. His outrage at what he considered to be Turnbull's inexcusable conduct prevented him from equating like with like. He said, 'Turnbull's lied to us all the way along the ...'

'Turnbull has merely not told *all* the truth.' I smiled, then added, 'The questions he was asked . . . they were about murder. He answered them. He answered them truthfully. That's my opinion. Questions concerning copulation weren't asked. Why the devil should he drag copulation into a conversation concerning murder?'

'It was rather more than "a conversation".'

'All right, an enquiry.'

'So, why copulation?'

'Exactly,' I nodded.

'Because – damn it all – the murder victims were prostitutes. Copulation was their business. And – damnation, Eddie, don't be so bloody blasé – he'd screwed 'em. It's *obvious*.'

'You'll make a fool of yourself,' I sighed.

'You've a twisted way of looking at things.'

'No.' I deliberately kept my voice under control. 'Ask a policeman the time – ask him directions – and he'll tell you. It's why he's there. They, too, have a specific purpose. It's why *they're* there. You – I – there are certain shops in Bordfield where we get things at trade price. The cinemas, we get in free. Perks of the job, Chris. Not bribery. Not blackmail. Every copper has *something*, because he's a copper. With Turnbull it was the use of whores.'

'That simple?' sneered Chris.

'That simple,' I assured him. 'We may not agree with his morals, but that doesn't make him a murderer.'

Chris couldn't (or wouldn't) see the sense of basic logic. He was still in a roaring temper when I left him and drove to the railway station to meet Mr Walters.

Railway stations. They – the whole railway network – are an unwanted legacy from the Victorian era. An ugly legacy which no amount of paint, no amount of alteration, no amount of speed, can make even moderately pleasant. They are echoing places which are either too empty or too full. They were never meant for moderation; at one moment they are near-deserted then the next moment, when a train pulls in, they are a babble of jostling, shouting, hurrying humanity. The buffet-cum-waiting-room as always reminded me of purgatory; a waiting place for undecided souls. I was there waiting for a train. I was there as a result of murder, and the eyes of every person in that room were shifty and haunted and could, without stretching the imagination too far, have been the eyes of a potential murderer. Frightened eyes. Guilty eyes. Waiting-room eyes.

I left the buffet-cum-waiting room and stood by the barrier until the Reading train arrived.

Despite the crush he was easily recognisable. The dark suit, the black tie, the tiny, overnight suitcase and the stooped shoulders all told their own story. Middle-aged – perhaps a little more than middle-aged – with close-cropped, greying hair and a figure which might once have been described as thickset, but which was now running to fat.

'Mr Walters?' I said.

'Eh?' For a moment he looked startled. Almost frightened. Then he muttered, 'Er – yes. That's me.'

'Police Inspector Caan.'

We shook hands, then I led him to the car.

The body had been removed to Kemington Royal Infirmary; the stark, white-tiled inhumanity of the public mortuary was no place in which to take a next-of-kin. There was a tiny, brick-built structure, standing apart from the infirmary complex: the so-called 'Chapel of Rest', built and used for this very purpose.

She was in a coffin – 'the shell' as it was unofficially called by policemen – a coffin in which cadavers were temporarily housed for identification purposes. I led him into the chapel and removed the silk square which covered her face – the silk square which had covered dozens of faces.

'Do you mind, Mr Walters?' I murmured. 'It's necessary, I'm afraid.'

He moved closer. He was trembling; his whole body shaking and his legs hardly able to hold him upright.

'It's necessary,' I repeated.

He shot a quick, furtive glance at the uncovered face, opened and closed his dry lips a couple of times, then said, 'No! No, it's not Emilia.'

'Mr Walters,' I said.

'It's not her.' He kept his face turned away from the coffin.

'They change,' I said brusquely. 'She's not asleep.'

'It's – it's not...'

'Look at her. *Look!*'

I think it must have been one of the worst moments of his life. Very slowly, very deliberately, he turned his head and, for all of five seconds, stared into the coffin. Then he nodded. Gently. With infinite sadness.

73

'It's – it's her,' he whispered. 'I'm sorry. Just for the moment, I . . . She looks different. That's all. Different, but it's my daughter.'

I replaced the silk square, guided him from the chapel and back to the car, then drove to a decent hotel for a drink and a mid-morning snack. As the meal progressed he began to pull himself together. The talk centred upon his daughter – which was natural enough – and the impression was that he was being held together by the rivets and glue of self-pity and self-deception. It irritated me. The truth was the truth and, one day, he'd learn the facts of his daughter's life via some scandal-splashed newspaper. It seemed right that he should be prepared.

He said, 'She was a good girl, Inspector Caan. A fine daughter.'

I grunted a non-committal reply.

'I don't know how her boss is going to manage.'

'Her boss?'

'She just about ran that office.'

'Which office?' I asked gently.

'Where she worked. The exporting firm. I know, she's said it so many times in her letters. I mean, y'know . . .' He moved a shoulder and tried to build up a smile of pride. 'Secretaries aren't easy to come by these days. And the money they were paying her. We were proud of her.'

'Samantha,' I murmured.

'Eh?'

'That's the name she worked under. Didn't she tell you *that*?'

'Samantha?' He scowled.

'She wasn't a secretary, Mr Walters.'

'How d'you mean. Every letter . . .'

'She was lying. I'm sorry, but she *was* lying.'

'Why would she lie? What's the point in her . . .'

'Mr Walters.' I kept my voice low, watched his face

74

and told him what he had to be told. 'Some damn news-paper will print it. You'd better hear it from me, then you *might* be able to keep it from her mother.'

'Go on.' His nostrils quivered slightly. His voice was harsh and threatening. He rasped, 'She's dead. She can't defend herself. But by Christ . . .'

'She was a prostitute,' I said flatly. 'Known as such. Convicted as such. Whatever lies she put in her letters, that's what she was. I realise this might come as a shock, but . . .'

Which, I fear, is when he threw the jug of near-boiling water in my face and, while I was temporarily blinded, knocked me unconscious.

I am told he used a chair. I am further told that it took three men to drag him away from me; that he went com-pletely berserk and would, without doubt, have killed me had he not been restrained.

This, as the courts would say, is pure hearsay evidence.

As far as I was concerned I regained consciousness in Kemington Royal Infirmary the next morning. I had required surgery for a broken jaw and a fractured skull and the word 'consciousness' is something of an exaggera-tion for the drug-befuddled state in which I remained for almost a week.

The ridiculous thing is that I was trying to do the man a favour and, whatever criticism the press may have made, my motives were beyond reproach. Unfortunately, there is no gentle way in which to tell a father that his murdered daughter was a professional whore. I knew this when I tried, but the information had to be given.

He was, of course, charged with Assault on Police. Harris visited me in hospital and, at my request, allowed this lesser charge rather than G.B.H. or Unlawful Wound-ing . . . a point which the press saw fit not to mention. In turn, the magistrates' court accepted his defence of 'great provocation' and placed him on probation for two years.

In short, it was a complete shambles and a gross miscarriage of justice. I was made out to be a villain and, as such, castigated by both local and national press.

While I was in hospital – indeed while my jaw was still wired – Chris visited me and, much to my disgust, adopted an attitude similar to that of the media.

'He didn't have to be told, you know,' he said.

Because of my jaw I wasn't able to talk, but I had a scribbling pad and pencil.

I glared at him, and scrawled –

The inquest?

'Evidence of identification, that's all. Opened, then adjourned. For God's sake, Eddie, you know the pattern.'

Why shouldn't he know? I wrote.

'Because he was already a broken man. It would have been kinder to let him live with his illusion.'

Told lies?

'Yes.' Chris nodded. 'There are times when you're very pompous, Eddie. And times when your pomposity touches cruelty. I don't want to lose your friendship, especially at a time like this, but don't ask me to feel too much sympathy. You've been hammered, but you deserved hammering.'

My hand trembled slightly as I wrote –

Piss off. I don't need your sympathy or friendship.

For a little more than three months I was away from the heart of things. First in hospital, then at home; first with stitches in my face and head and wires in my jaw, then being fed a gradually decreasing dosage of analgesics as the deep-rooted pains eased.

A month after the Bowling Side killings they were no longer news. Even in the local newspaper they moved from

76

the front page, then deserved a single paragraph and finally disappeared from print altogether. I lay in my bed, or sat in a cushioned chair, and visualised the gradual spinning down of the enquiry. At its height, the hunt had skimmed almost a hundred officers from other duties, but at a guess that hundred had been reduced to about a dozen if that after the first four weeks of activity. Only so many people can be questioned. Only so many questions can be asked. Every enquiry is finite; there comes a point when everything that *can* be done *has* been done. I estimated that that point had been reached at about four weeks after the murders.

For a fortnight – perhaps three weeks – nothing whatever was printed about the stranglings in the newspapers, then once more there were headlines.

Turnbull had been arrested and charged.

I was still off duty and at home when the case reached the crown court. I could, I suppose, have invited one or more of my colleagues to the house and pumped them for information. Equally, I could have visited Kemington D.H.Q. and learned the facts first hand. Indeed there was nothing to prevent me from attending the Crown Court hearing in order to listen to the evidence as it was presented.

I did none of these things. The truth is I was aware that I was (at least to some degree) *persona non grata* with my police colleagues. It hurt a little. I didn't blame Chris – I still don't blame Chris – but I was acutely conscious of the fact that if Chris, my friend, had held me in such low esteem as a result of my telling Walters the truth, those who were not my friends would take pleasure in being openly offensive. I had no desire to court insults before it was necessary, therefore I contented myself with buying a good selection of reliable newspapers and from them reading the various twists and turns of the trial.

77

Turnbull had been a fool. That at least. He had demanded too many perquisites from the whores of Bowling Side. The damn fool had had something of a crush on the Walters woman and had, at one time, suggested that she leave the streets and set up home with him. She'd refused, obviously: once a whore, always a whore. Turnbull had threatened her. More than that, he'd threatened her in the presence of the Hewitt woman.

She in turn had threatened to expose his quasi-corruptions to his senior officers and via them to his wife.

As the newspapers told it, it was a pretty ragged prosecution; little more than a procession of confessed harlots following each other into the witness box each eager to scrape a little of the tarnish from her own image and smear it upon Turnbull's reputation. Turnbull *could* have committed the murders; that in effect was the argument of the prosecution. The evidence of the street women merely provided a possible motive.

Turnbull, of course, pleaded 'Not Guilty' and (a purely personal opinion) any advocate worthy of the name would have demolished the case for the prosecution to at least the point where that element of 'reasonable doubt' was very evident. As it was (again my own opinion, from my reading of the newspapers) too many wrong questions were asked in cross-examination and, where the appropriate questions *were* asked, they were never pressed home to the point where the witness might have been broken.

But who knows?

Who can *ever* predict the findings of a jury?

Turnbull was convicted and sentenced to 'life' imprisonment, which I have no doubt the judge expected to be the usual ten or eleven years before the granting of parole.

Nevertheless, the case sickened me. I knew Harris. I knew Warlock. A prolonged session with either, or both, and a weak man – and Turnbull was that – could be made to contradict himself on minor details, and from those contradictions could be held up as a liar in all things.

The trial lasted three days and during that time, while not harping on it constantly, Mother, Aunt Elizabeth and I discussed it frequently. (At this period the wire had been removed from my jaw and, although eating solids remained a slow and rather painful process, speech was no longer a problem.)

We were talking about it one day the three of us. It was one evening. We were settled around a warm fire and outside the wind was rising and slashing the rain against the curtained windows. I remember it was very cosy, very comfortable, not at all the atmosphere in which to discuss the twin topics of murder and lasciviousness.

Mother said, 'Turnbull. A weak man, I think.'

'A damn fool,' I remarked.

Aunt Elizabeth – dear, innocent Aunt Elizabeth – said, 'The poor man, though. And his poor wife.'

'A man,' I said bluntly, 'is never entitled to false respect. He's a fornicator. A lecher. I see no reason why the world should hold him in esteem.'

'He's not alone,' remarked Mother.

'Indeed he's not alone. The man Stone, another married man, every bit as immoral as Turnbull. On his own admission he visits Henry's café solely for the purpose of picking up whores. He was there on the . . .'

I stopped speaking. Suddenly. Like the switching off of a radio.

Mother saw the expression on my face and said 'Edmund?'

'It doesn't matter,' I muttered.

'It certainly *looks* as if it matters.'

'Stone's a liar,' I said.

'I'm sorry. I don't . . .'

'It doesn't matter. It's unimportant.' I waved her

question aside. 'He's just a liar, that's all. A liar as well as a whoremonger.'

In retrospect I have to ask myself certain questions.

The officer, Turnbull, was on trial therefore why didn't I contact Chris and explain the inconsistencies of Stone's story? Why did I dismiss such an obvious untruth – if indeed it *was* an untruth and not a mistake – as unimportant? Why at that moment did I decide to do nothing?

Resentment perhaps? An unwillingness on my part to make a first move towards mending the rift between Chris and myself?

This, I think, was part of it; probably a large part. But the main reason was that, by exposing Stone as a liar, little could be done to help Turnbull. Turnbull had been sentenced and was now in prison. The law had taken its course. And the law, although rarely wrong was almost impossible to reverse. Turnbull was guilty because the law *said* he was guilty. The law is a very stiff-necked animal and only in extreme circumstances will it admit to making a mistake.

The lie?

Henry, if you recall, had admitted that the murdered Walters woman had visited his eating-house at about nine o'clock on the evening of the murder. She'd been with a man called 'Alfred' . . . obviously Alfred Stone. They had, according to Henry stayed for about thirty minutes. Chris had questioned him hard and, without much doubt, he'd have mentioned any subsequent visit to the eating-house by either Walters or Stone.

Stone on the other hand, and under close questioning in an interview room, had admitted visiting Henry's place *. . . at just before or about midnight.*

More than two hours – almost *three* hours – were unaccounted for.

Unaccounted for? Or had somebody been lying? Or had somebody made a mistake? The last seemed least probable; the interviewing had taken place within hours of the murder and, although a few minutes either way could be an accepted difference between two people's estimate of a given time, two hours (almost three hours) was ridiculous. The chances were that either Stone or Henry had been lying.

Why? Why should they lie?

I had little to do and time to spare, therefore I wrestled for answers to these questions.

Why should Henry lie? Why (if he *was* lying) should he place Stone and the Walters woman together in his eating-house at nine o'clock? Why should he *not* place them there at midnight?

I could come up with no answer, other that is than that Henry was a raving lunatic who didn't know the time of day to within two hours!

And Stone?

Stone was a different problem. It was possible – indeed the only possibility with any sanity attached – that Stone wasn't lying; that the atmosphere of the interview room and the harshness of the questioning had forced the truth from him. An unwilling truth, perhaps. It then needed but a small step and a suspicious mind to move to another possibility. That Henry's lie had been told as a favour to Stone; that (originally) Stone had wanted it to be thought that he and the Walters woman had been in the eating-house some two or three hours before the *real* time they were there.

Which meant . . .

I wasn't sure what it meant.

Those three months. I toyed with so many ideas. I thought so many thoughts, dreamed so many dreams, schemed so many schemes. I went for long walks during the convalescent period, often into and around Bowling Side. The infernal place fascinated me. As far as I was concerned it embodied everything I loathed. Everything I detested. And yet it drew me, like a stoat draws a terrified rabbit.

No! That analogy is utterly wrong.

I was no rabbit. If anything, I was the stoat. Bowling Side was *my* police area. My responsibility. My battle and my victory. For seven heartbreaking years I'd fought its compound of evils and in all that time I'd refused to become sullied by its filth.

Nevertheless...

Perhaps I'd had enough. Perhaps in the long term *it* had beaten *me*. It wasn't impossible. I was no drag-'em-out-and-kick-their-teeth-in police officer. My battles were fought quietly and systematically. In the end, I'd won, but not necessarily with flying banners. Often I was the only person who knew I'd won. It wasn't a hollow victory, but it *was* a victory for which I was never given credit.

The question of rank also arose.

The rank of uniformed inspector. Common usage accepted it as a stepping stone; a man or a woman had to be an inspector before he or she could become a chief inspector, and from there a superintendent. Simple inspectorship was a mere staging post, en route for higher things.

But not with me, it seemed.

I tried to be objective. I tried to recall any fellow-officer who held the rank of uniformed inspector for seven years; at the same section and without so much as a hint of advancement. I could think of nobody. A handful – no more than half a dozen – had been promoted from sergeant to inspector at some time within the last five years of their service, as an official bonus for a job well done... an increase in pay and, more important, an increase in pension. But as far as I was concerned that didn't apply.

I had another decade of policing ahead of me. Ten years and – as things stood – ten more years as an inspector in charge of Bowling Side.

To change the metaphor. Grammatically speaking the rank of uniformed inspector was a mere comma within the overall sentence of a police career. But it would seem with me it had been converted into a full stop.

Thus I seriously contemplated resignation.

Until, that is, Harris visited me . . .

Harris. His full official rank was and still is Assistant Chief Constable (Crime) Bordfield Region. He was and still is what every television viewer imagines a top-ranking detective should look like.

All my life I'd hated men like Harris. I'd detested their monumental self-esteem, their bulldozer mannerisms, their refusal to admit of weakness in themselves and their open contempt for weakness in others.

He lacked even the common courtesy to telephone; to ask whether he might, or even inform me that he was going to, visit me. He merely arrived on the front doorstep one afternoon about three weeks before I expected to resume duty and that he was there at all was meant to be taken as an honour.

Aunt Elizabeth offered him tea and buttered scones and he accepted with all the arrogance of God Almighty accepting the offer of Moses to carry the tablets. We sat in silence waiting for the arrival of the tea and scones. Silence, but an odd silence. I was about to say 'The silence of a tomb', yet that would have been not merely a cliché, but also very wrong. There was nothing dead about that silence. Indeed, it almost vibrated with life; with mutual dislike. It was rather like the silence which precedes an artillery duel.

When we were alone I waited. *He'd* come to *me*. It was

a slight advantage, and if possible I was going to use it.

'You'll be back in uniform in a couple of weeks or so,' he growled.

'According to the medics,' I agreed.

'That's why I'm here.'

I didn't answer. My role was not that of making things easy for him.

He said, 'Bowling Side.'

I still didn't answer.

'We were wondering whether it might be wise.'

'We?'

'Me,' he admitted grudgingly. 'A change of venue, perhaps.'

'Why?' I asked softly.

'Damn it all, Caan. You don't think you're popular there, do you?'

'I never was.'

'That's what I mean. I think...'

'Since when did popularity have much to do with police work?'

He breathed a little more heavily.

I added, 'I don't have to tell *you* of all people. You don't give a damn whether you're popular or not. In fact – correct me if I'm wrong – you don't *want* to be popular with a certain class of people.'

Once more there was a silence. I had the feeling that I'd done the near-impossible. I'd backed the great Harris into a corner, and he didn't like it. The solemnity of his expression darkened. He almost scowled.

'I could arrange a transfer to another station,' he rumbled.

'You could arrange a *proposed* transfer,' I corrected him. 'I could refuse it. You'd then have to justify it for it to take effect.' I allowed my lips to relax into a quick, tight smile. 'The days of moving police officers around like pawns on a chessboard – and for no good reason – are past, Mr Harris. You know it. I know it.' I paused, then asked, 'What justification would you give?'

'Warlock's had a complete clear-out.'

'And nobody's objected?'

'Nobody,' he grunted.

'In that case, I'd be the first.'

'In God's name why?' He glared at me. 'Do you like the bloody place so much?'

'Promotion?' I asked gently.

'Eh?'

'This transfer you're here to talk about. Does it carry a chief-inspectorship?'

'No.'

'I thought not.' I placed my cup on the coffee table, leaned back in my chair and said, 'Mr Harris, let me put *my* position. I don't like Bowling Side. Nobody in his right mind would. But just because a couple of tarts have been strangled doesn't intimidate *me*. I happen to have told the father of one of those tarts the unvarnished truth, nor does *that* intimidate me. The truth, it would seem, hurts. It embarrasses people. It makes friends call you "pompous". It makes superintendents adopt new-broom tactics. It even makes assistant chief constables visit the home of a lowly uniformed inspector and, for no good reason, suggest that that inspector should accept a transfer without the accompanying promotion.'

I paused, then continued, 'You've had a wasted journey, Mr Harris. My respects to Superintendent Warlock, but here's one member of Kemington Division who'll *not* be moving. I'll fight a proposed transfer all the way up to the Chief Constable, if nececessary. All the way up to the Home Office. Give me one good reason why I should accept that transfer – one reason *I* accept as valid – and I'll ...'

FOUR

These infernal machines!

However, it isn't important. Suffice to say that Harris couldn't budge me. Warlock sulked a little and even went out of his way to be nasty, but I shrugged his ill-mannerisms off and took up the reins of Bowling Side where I'd left them. I even tightened them a little. I sensed from the first an undercurrent of antagonism; something more than the usual 'feeling out' of a senior officer new to this recently transferred batch of men and sergeants. There was a surliness. A mistrust. And I didn't give a damn.

Tallboy, if you recall, had once accused me of lacking hatred. Of being 'too decent' to be a successful police officer.

How wrong he was!

I can hate. I could always hate. But unlike most men I can hide my hatred; control it; use it, as a means to an end.

Those first few weeks back on duty were proof of that. The men under me refused to respect me. The men over me went out of their way to be objectionable. Therefore I fought back, *hard*.

To Warlock and Perkins I was coldly correct. I refused them even surface friendship. I gave them mock-respect and made damn sure they *knew* it was mock-respect, but equally made damn sure it was not obvious enough to call for official complaint.

To the sergeants and constables of Bowling Side I was a deliberate bastard. I demanded everything – everything! – 'by the book'. Laxity was something they daren't even attempt. I wanted to know exactly where every man was every minute of his working day, *exactly* where he was. And if he was where he shouldn't be, or wasn't where he should be, I wanted an explanation – in writing.

An inspector in charge of a section can do that. He can make it hard or he can make it easy. If, like me, he pulls out all the stops he can make it hell.

About a week after I'd returned to duty, Chris visited the section on some enquiry or another – some theft, I think – and tentatively at first, then with growing confidence patched up our broken friendship.

'Back in harness,' he observed.

'Obviously.'

His half-smile was an invitation which at first I saw no reason to accept.

'Back in working order.'

'Otherwise, I wouldn't be here.'

'Oh – er – no ... of course not.'

We were in my office. He'd entered without knocking. This in itself had annoyed me, until I remembered that in the past neither of us had considered it necessary to ask for, or receive, an invitation to enter our respective sanctums.

'Coffee?' he suggested.

I glanced at my watch and said, 'The cadet should be bringing me one in about ten minutes.'

'No, I mean decent coffee. The Park Restaurant.'

'I'm a busy man.'

'It won't run away,' he said gently.

'What?'

'All that paperwork. It'll still be there when you come back.'

'It and more with it.'

'Eddie.' He smiled and frowned at the same time. 'Cut it out, eh? We're both grown men.'

87

'I have,' I said grimly, 'certain tigers – and not paper tigers, hungry tigers – snapping at my heels.'

'I know.' The smile broadened and the frown disappeared. 'Sod 'em for ten minutes. Let's hide ourselves.'

Chris, it must be admitted, could be a tempter. He had a charm which, when he turned it on at full power, was almost irresistible. And the truth was I was feeling the strain a little. I wasn't seeking popularity – I'd never sought popularity – but open belligerency can become boring and even soul-sapping after a time. I was, I suspect, in need of a friend. One friend, no more. One man to whom I could speak openly.

For whatever reason, I agreed and together we strolled to The Park Restaurant.

The Park Restaurant. It was and still is just that; a restaurant at the entrance to Bowling Side Park.

That Bowling Side *had* a park was a minor miracle. It was on the very fringe of the section : a comparatively tiny open space which a munificent local authority had designated as a token lung via which this area of grime and outrageously high-density built-up shambles might, perhaps, breathe. During the day the kids used it as a cricket or football pitch. After dark (assuming they could find space enough between the dog shit) couples used it for copulation.

Strangely for Bowling Side the Park Restaurant was a neat but unpretentious little café. It did not make the common mistake of being too ambitious. It served tea or coffee with cakes or sandwiches, nothing more. But the crockery was clean and unchipped and the table-linen unstained and freshly laundered. At a guess, it just about provided the middle-aged couple who ran it with a moderate income; it was never busy, but on the other hand it was rarely deserted.

We found a corner table private and beyond talking-distance from the mother and child who were the restaurant's only other customers. We sipped coffee, we smoked cigarettes and, for a while, we spliced the broken ends of our friendship : I asked after Chris's wife and he, in turn, enquired about Mother and Aunt Elizabeth. There was no need for mock-melodrama – no need for apologies or handshaking – we were back to the old relationship and we both accepted the fact without further comment.

Then Chris smiled and said, 'You're earning a reputation, Eddie.'

I nodded. I knew what he meant.

'Is it necessary?' he asked quietly.

'I think so,' I sighed.

'Why?'

'Harris visited me while I was off duty,' I said.

He raised interested eyebrows.

'A certain amount of subtle leaning,' I explained. 'A proposed transfer from here, but without promotion.'

'Which you refused.'

'Which I refused,' I agreed. I drew on my cigarette, then said, 'I have them all, Chris. Harris, Warlock – the lot – all watching for the wrong step.'

'It's a reaction,' he said heavily.

'To what?' I quite genuinely didn't understand.

'Turnbull,' he said. 'A copper commits murder. Double murder. One rotten apple – a *very* rotten apple – the natural thing is to empty the whole bloody barrel, just in case.'

'If he did,' I murmured.

'Turnbull?' Chris stared.

'He was tried and found guilty,' I said.

'Which means . . .'

'Which means he was tried and found guilty.'

'Meaning?' Chris was floundering a little.

89

'Just that.' I smiled. 'He didn't confess, did he?'

'No. But ...'

'Nobody actually *saw* him commit the murders.'

'For Christ's sake, Eddie.'

'Let us,' I said, 'assume he didn't. Let us assume that this great English Legal System of ours actually *can* make a mistake. Not too wild an assumption ... it's made enough mistakes in the past.'

'You think Turnbull's innocent?' Poor Chris was almost open-mouthed at the suggestion.

'I think,' I said grimly, 'that until we're sure – until *everybody's* sure – those apples in that barrel you're talking about ought not to be slung on the compost heap.'

Chris said, 'Eddie, everybody *is* sure.'

'Not everybody. *I'm* not.'

A couple of times in that *tête-à-tête* which re-established our friendship I was tempted to mention the time discrepancy in Stone's and Henry's stories. I didn't. Perhaps it would have been – what? Dangerous? Perhaps I didn't want to flush a false hare and make myself look too much of a fool. Perhaps a dozen reasons. Perhaps no reason at all.

It matters not. I was sad about Turnbull and, had I thought for one moment that the time difference between Stone's version and Henry's version of what happened on the night of the Walters woman's killing would have helped, I might have mentioned it.

I didn't, let's leave it at that.

Meanwhile it was coming up to Christmas; the nights were getting colder and longer; the idiot fraternity of Bowling Side seemed to be getting more drunken and more rowdy, as if rehearsing for the annual orgy of booze and fornication.

Then four days before Christmas the third street-woman was found strangled.

It was, I don't have to remind you, a great day for the media.

Elsie Golders was viewed as somebody 'special'. Special? I fear that, as far as I was concerned, she was one more harlot. Younger than the first two, not yet thirty, but other than that in no way different. As a teenager she'd touched near-fame as an 'up-and-coming' pop singer. She had, I learned, appeared on television a few times; one of those countless, faceless, soon-forgotten female fillers-in who space out the standard format of most comedy shows.

Alive she had been one of scores. Dead she became unique.

On the streets she used her old stage-name. 'Ruby Koar.' A stupid, senseless name : one wonders where the fools who determine the destiny of these youngsters find these ridiculous names. But 'Ruby Koar' was the name she used as a singer and the name the newspapers gave her as a corpse.

And, oh, the flurry when Warlock found the body. Warlock, of all people. Warlock the incorruptible. Warlock, whose waking life seemed to be devoted to the task of seeking out faults in my manner of running Bowling Side. It was, you must agree, poetic justice to perfection.

I was on the street; I spent most of my time on the street in those days, chasing the patrolling constables and sergeants, ensuring that they kept on their toes and did nothing for which I might be held responsible. It was almost one o'clock in the morning when the message came over my car radio. Warlock would be meeting me at one-thirty by the canal bridge.

I was waiting for him, but he never arrived.

At a few minutes after two o'clock, the car radio broke the news and, I must confess, I chuckled quietly. The biter had been well and truly bit.

On the road to the bridge – near the entrance to Benning's Yard – he'd seen the glove on the pavement. The white glove about a foot from the kerb-edge. It had caught the glow of his headlights. At first he'd thought it was a hand; a gruesome thing; a hand severed at the wrist. Such was the atmosphere in Bowling Side at that time. Warlock thought it was a *hand*! One can, I think, imagine the tingling of his nape hairs, the constriction of his throat, the sudden dryness of his mouth. Warlock: the would-be-perfectionist. Harris's catspaw in the hounding of me from the section I refused to leave.

He'd stopped his car, investigated, and almost stumbled across the legs of the dead woman where she was propped against the wall in the darkened entrance to Benning's Yard.

I drove to the scene, and all hell was let loose!

Harris, Lennox and Chris were already there. The Bowling Siders were milling around like a football crowd. Squad cars, panda vans and foot-patrol officers were arriving continuously. The two previous murders had been nothing – mere run-ups – to this third, but you see, *this* corpse had been found by a police superintendent. Not a police constable this time. It was like grand opera as opposed to *lieder*.

I busied myself handling the growing number of ghoulish rubber-neckers. The newspapermen, and later the people from television and radio, I passed on to Harris. He was the one who'd backed Warlock in Warlock's 'clean sweep' scheme, he was the one best able to justify that scheme.

The sky was lightening towards dawn before Chris

could disentangle himself from the core of the activity and snatch a few words, and a quiet smoke, with me within the shelter of my own car.

'Strewth!' He blew out his cheeks in mock-amazement. 'How many more dead slags have you tucked away in this bloody section of yours?'

'Not Turnbull this time,' I murmured.

'On *that* process of elimination we're in for one hell of a slog.'

'Warlock?' I suggested mischievously.

'Eh?' His eyes widened.

'He found her, he killed her. That was, more or less, the basis of the prosecution of Turnbull.'

'Oh, come *on*.' For the moment he took my suggestion seriously. 'Turnbull had motive. A lot of motive.'

'Every man,' I reminded him, 'who ever went with a disease-ridden trollop has the same motive, which makes it no motive at all.'

'You really think Turnbull was innocent?' He looked at me quizzically. 'Just between us two, you really think that?'

'I think it was a poor case.'

'That's not quite the same thing.'

'I also think Warlock was gunning for him. Your boss, too, Harris. They had to have a whipping-boy. They chose Turnbull.'

'For Christ's sake, Eddie! That's...'

'That's what I think,' I said gruffly. 'You asked. That's my answer. The cards fell badly for Turnbull. The damn fool gave them a motive... of sorts.'

'He's innocent in other words?'

'There's a hell of a lot more than "reasonable doubt". In my mind, at least. Let's put it that way.'

That's the way the talk went. That's the way talk often goes when policemen who are friends chat quietly together.

I didn't expect to convince Chris. Who *ever* convinces another man against his own beliefs? And yet I think I sowed doubt.

For my own sake I daren't do more.

I recall I expounded, more than a little, upon hatred. It was towards the end of our conversation. We'd talked about this latest killing and I'd mentioned the fact that Warlock had been on his way to keep an appointment with me when he'd found the body. Talk of Warlock, as far as I was concerned, was a natural lead-in to talk of hatred.

I said, 'The man's a climber. A creeper. He can hate for no better reason than that it might please one of his superiors. That's about the only reason he has for hating me. And yet he *does* hate me. Openly. Without qualification. I bucked Harris, ergo Warlock hates my guts. That's a damn-fool reason if ever there was one. But it's all Warlock needs. It's good enough reason for *him*. What the hell does that make him, Chris?'

'A louse,' said Chris simply. Then added, 'If it's true.'

'A louse,' I agreed. 'And don't ever doubt the truth of it.'

'In that case . . .' Chris smiled, shrugged, screwed out his cigarette in the dashboard ashtray and climbed from the car to join the group at the heart of the incident.

That morning, as I caught up with some loss of sleep, I dreamed about Turnbull. It was a most vivid dream. Vivid, and yet meaningless.

Via some twist of the subconscious Turnbull was chief constable. Not of this force; of some unknown, unidentified, force, but not of *this* force. A happy man, forever laughing. But strange, idiot laughter. The laughter of a man without a complete mind, and yet not particularly frightening.

94

And he was my friend.

Much of the dream I have lost, but this I remember very clearly. That Turnbull was very much my friend. And, moreover, a friend with great power. Far more power than any earthly chief constable. Whatever I wanted, I could have. Whatever it was. Nor did I have to ask . . . merely *want*. He seemed to have some trick of mind-reading. He seemed to *know* without being told.

A strange dream. In many ways a dream more real than reality. And, like so many dreams, touched with a fore-telling of the immediate future.

I was awakened by a tapping on the bedroom door. The door opened a few inches and Aunt Elizabeth's voice called, 'Eddie!'

'Yes?' I raised myself on one elbow.

'A telephone message, dear. There's a meeting – a con-ference of some kind – at the chief constable's office. Four o'clock. They'd like you to attend.'

His name was (is) Gilliant. Chief Constable Gilliant. Part rumour, part fact, I suppose, but gossip has it that he climbed to what is believed to be the second-highest-paid police job in the U.K. via the hard route. From constable to C.I.D., to Regional Crime Squad, to assistant chief constable, through various chief constableships, and now chief constable of the Lessford Metropolitan Police District.

I'd met him three – probably four – times before, and always the word 'dedication' sprang to mind. Not 'fanatic-ism': there was about him that cold, clinical objective-ness which no fanatic ever has. A frightening man, but not a vicious man. A cool man, but not a cold man. A solitary man, but not a lonely man. These are the nuances by means of which I estimated him. By means of which I still estimate him.

The office was large, even luxurious, but one must presume *all* chief constable's offices are large and luxurious. It was certainly large enough to hold and seat us all without any feeling of claustrophobia. Gilliant was there, of course. So were Harris, Lennox and Warlock. Chris and myself made up the half-dozen.

Why me?

I pondered the question myself. Possibly as a gesture. Possibly as a representative of rank; superintendents, chief superintendents and assistant chief constables were represented by Warlock, Lennox and Harris, the grass-roots C.I.D. was represented by Chris. It is possible that the crumb of acknowledgement made to the uniformed rank and file was my own inclusion in the conference.

Gilliant opened the discussion. There were no frills. No gentle lead-in. He spoke quietly, but with supreme authority.

He said, 'We have a multi-sided problem, gentlemen. The murder of Elsie Golders, the fact that she is the third prostitute to be murdered in the same district within months, and the fact that all three women were strangled – which presupposes a single killer. Your opinions and suggestions, please.'

'Bowling Side, sir,' said Warlock. He made it sound as if that was the *answer*. More . . . the answer to every problem posed.

'Bowling Side is a police section, Mr Warlock.' Gilliant's voice pinned Warlock's stupidity to the card of hard fact, as surely as if it was a moth straight from the killing-bottle. 'A police section, as such, is no reason for murder or are you suggesting it *is*?'

'No, sir, but . . .'

'Somebody in Bowling Side doesn't like prostitutes,' interrupted Harris gruffly.

I hesitated for a second, then said, 'In that case somebody's in prison who *shouldn't* be.'

'Precisely.' Gilliant moved his lips into a quick, tight smile. 'Our problem, gentlemen. Our *real* problem.'

'Carbon-copy?' suggested Lennox quietly.

'Possible,' agreed Gilliant.

Harris growled, 'More than likely.'

Gilliant said, 'No, I wouldn't put it higher than "possible", Mr Harris.'

'Turnbull was convicted, sir,' said Warlock.

'It wouldn't be the first mistaken conviction, Superintendent.' Chris spoke for the first time. Credit to him; he flew his colours alongside mine and against those of his own superintendent and his own assistant chief constable. He added, 'At the very least, the Walters and the Hewitt files should be reopened.'

'At the very least,' agreed Gilliant.

That was the way Gilliant guided the discussion, if indeed it *was* a discussion. As it progressed, I began to have doubts. Equally, it could have been a deliberate ploy on the part of the chief constable to gather all the main parties together and, from their own mouths, allow them to convict themselves. Warlock came out of it badly. So, for that matter, did Harris. Without being made to look blundering fools they were certainly forced into an admission of hasty decision-making.

Harris almost snarled, 'The bloody morals of the man. He was...'

'Mr Harris, you don't really mean what you're implying, I'm sure.' Gilliant raised warning eyebrows. 'Turnbull was charged – and convicted – of murder, not immorality.'

'Immorality ain't yet a crime.' Lennox had looked worried and spoken little. He rumbled, 'It's one hell of a thought, though, ain't it? That old Turnbull was sent to nick for immorality disguised as murder. That's the trouble with courts o' law. Always has been.' He rubbed the back of his podgy neck ruefully. 'That's what they call themselves, courts o' law. Morals don't enter into it. Every ruddy judge I've ever known always goes on about that – that morals don't effect the issue – that's when he's gonna moralise like the clappers.'

'You sent him down, Chief Superintendent,' said Warlock nastily.

'Aye.' Lennox nodded solemnly. 'But *you're* the one that's now so bloody sure.'

The journey back to Bowling Side Police Station was less charged with expectancy than had been the journey to Lessford Headquarters. I'd travelled out with Chris and Lennox shared our return journey – he'd travelled from Bordfield with Harris.

As we neared the outskirts of Lessford, Lennox leaned forward from the rear seat and said, 'What's he like, Inspector?'

'Turnbull?' I knew the question had been addressed to me.

'What sort of a bloke is he?'

'Normal.' I paused, then added, 'I'd have said conscientious.'

'Once upon a time?'

I nodded.

'There's no evidence,' said Chris, 'that he shafted prozzies in duty time.'

'A sort o' hobby?' suggested Lennox.

'What I'm getting at, sir . . .'

'I know what you're getting at, Tallboy, old son. You're like me. You're leaning over backwards, trying to be fair now it's too flaming late.'

I muttered, 'Don't blame Turnbull. Off duty, on duty: don't blame, Turnbull.'

'For killing 'em?'

'No, sir. For the other thing.'

'For being a lecherous hound?'

'It's their job, sir. It's their profession.' I sought to convince this obese detective chief superintendent of the truth. 'It's the old Eve-and-the-apple bit. They know it's wrong – they know damn well it's wrong – but their job's to tempt. Their job's to tart it up. Make it look almost respectable. A bit on the side. Virility. All that sort of crap.'

'You don't like 'em,' he observed.

'No,' I agreed. 'I've heard it argued they're a necessity. For my money they're a blasted nuisance, period.'

'You've enough of 'em at Bowling Side,' he observed. 'You should be something of an expert.'

'I am,' I agreed bluntly.

Little more was said on the subject. Lennox outlined the general strategy of the enquiry; virtually a repeat of the Walters and Hewitt murder hunts.

'Those bloody files,' he muttered. 'We'll have to have 'em out again and fine-tooth-comb 'em. We might have missed summat.'

I quaked a little. That two-hour-plus time discrepancy. They'd find it. Nothing surer. And I'd known about it forever, or so it seemed. And I'd kept silent, which had been a damn-fool thing to do. Then they'd dig, and dig . . .

'All convicted prostitutes,' mused Lennox. 'All strangled. All left with summat near the corpse to attract attention : the shoe, the coat, the glove. Anything else in common?'

'All found by coppers?' suggested Chris.

'All found by coppers,' agreed Lennox.

The obvious was voiced and repeated, with gaps of thoughtful silence between.

I asked, 'Chris and I . . . we work together again?'

'Why not?' muttered Lennox.

'Superintendent Warlock . . .' I began.

'I'll handle Warlock.'

I nodded my satisfaction.

'Start tonight,' said Lennox. 'Dig deep, *bloody* deep. If anybody's as much as farted out of tune I want to know about it. This time we have to be sure.'

A crude way of putting it? Lennox's way. But both Chris and I knew what he meant. That same night we scoured the streets of Bowling Side asking questions. Taking non-answers and recording them. Arranging for questionees to call at the resurrected Incident Centre and there tape their stories on to a cassette, to be typed out later, then given to them to read and sign.

Do you? Have you? Can you? Will you? How many questions we started with those words. Blunt questions. Devious questions. Questions disguised as simple statements. Questions asked behind a façade of personal opinion. A question can be asked a score of different ways and we used each way to ask hundreds of questions.

Bowling Side didn't (still doesn't) sleep. While decent citizens were abed, the scum of Bowling Side sauntered the streets looking for custom and the custom was there. Prowling cars. Men with shifty, half-ashamed eyes seeking vice and perversion.

And yet . . .

The first hard frost of the year seemed to harden and make brittle the air of those shabby streets. Seemed to purify and make clean. Seemed to halt the decay and sweep aside the shame. It countered our weariness and kept us sharp, even in the small hours. Therefore we could feel the hidden atmosphere of fear. The street-women paused slightly in their steady walk as we approached, and we noticed. It required the sight of a warrant card to make them relax and then, when they recognised us as their 'guardians', they seemed unwilling to leave us. Three of their kind were dead and death was something even *they* feared. They almost sighed with relief when, as we talked, a duo of uniformed constables, with which Bowling Side had been swamped, turned a corner and walked slowly along a pavement.

Chris remarked, 'We're only short of a pea-souper,' and I knew what he meant without explanation.

Bowling Side. Whitechapel. The man who strangled whores. Jack the Ripper. The equation was too obvious to need explanation. I felt the sweet terror of Annie Chapman's Dorset Street, of Marie Kelly's Miller Court, of Fashion Street and Flower and Dean Street, and Thrawl Street, of Victorian England and the most evil streets in the whole of the United Kingdom.

Indeed, all we were short of was a 'pea-souper'.

It was well after one o'clock in the morning when we ended up at Henry's Place. It was, I suppose, the logical climax; we'd worked our way steadily through as disgusting a mixture of pimps, harlots, madams, landlady's and police snouts as it was possible to find; we'd been cursed, buttered-up-to, conned and fawned upon until I, for one, was even more sickened than usual by the human race. All I needed to complete the night's collection was Henry.

Presumably Chris felt the same.

'Clear 'em.' Chris jerked his head at the scattering of customers littering the tables.

'Look, you can't . . .'

'Don't tell me what I *can't* do,' snapped Chris, 'otherwise I'll bloody soon demonstrate what I *can*.'

That was our mood. That was our temper. Unfortunately for him, Henry was there to catch the sting in the tail of the night's questioning. He had sense enough to know when he was treading on dangerous ground; he cleared the eating-house with ill grace, but he cleared it without further protest.

Chris gathered us around one of the stained tables; two inquisitors and a squirming victim, seated on three cheap and unsteady chairs. And never before had I been party to the brand of interrogation suffered by the unfortunate Henry. Chris's voice was as jagged, as uncompromising, as broken glass and I tried to match him tone for tone. Between us we slashed Henry to shreds.

He was already sweating and crouching in his chair when Chris said, 'Okay. Let's go back a few months. The first two.'

'The – the first . . .'

'Walters. Hewitt.'

'For God's sake. Turnbull's . . .'

'Forget Turnbull,' I interrupted.

'Two men here,' said Chris, 'weren't on the jury.'

'Y'mean . . .'

'The talk,' said Chris.

'W-what talk?'

'Walters and Hewitt. There'll have been talk.'

'Y'mean, since the trial?'

'I mean talk. Any sort of talk.'

'I – I dunno.'

'They don't sit here like dummies.'

'No. But . . .'

'They talk.'

'Yes. But . . .'

'You listen.'

'Not always. Not . . .'

'What do they talk about?'

'Things. Y'know . . .' Henry spread his hands. 'Things.'

'Walters?'

'I – I reckon. Sometimes.'

'Hewitt?'

'Y'know . . . Sometimes.'

'Do they think Turnbull killed Walters and Hewitt?' asked Chris.

'Some – er – some do. Some don't. Most of 'em couldn't care.' He ended in a rush and said, 'They don't *now.*'

'Stone?' I suggested gently.

'What about Stone?' Henry stared.

Chris said, 'Hold it.'

'What?'

'You didn't know his second name last time we asked.'

'Oh!'

'And you lied,' I added.

Why does a man do it? The question I've asked myself so many times. Why does a man deliberately walk thin ice? For the kick? For the thrill? To test his own reaction to danger?

Or is there a deeper, more profound reason?

God knows, God knows why I did it at that time and in that way.

But by three o'clock when we returned to the clean chill of the streets we had the answer. Such a simple answer: so puerile as to be almost undeserving of the question.

Henry and Stone were cousins . . . as simple as *that.* Cousins who knew each other well; cousins who shared the secret of Stone's excursions into professional copulation. And Henry knew his cousin. Knew him to be at least *capable* of murder. The lie about the time when Stone and the Walters whore had been in the eating-house had been a cousinly cover-up, just in case. Stone, according to a near-tearful Henry, *could* have been the murderer. Could have been and at the time, as far as

Henry was concerned, *was*. A slut like Walters. A man with a temper like Stone's. Jesus Christ, he *could* have been, so easily.

'Bloody magnificent!' growled Chris as we walked to where we'd parked the car. 'Talk about being back at square one.'

'Stone?' I asked quietly.

'We checked the taxi firm. They verified Stone's statement. Unless he's come up with some fancy dodge we know damn-all about . . .' He sighed and ended, 'Not Stone.'

'Turnbull?' I murmured.

'You have this thing about Turnbull, Eddie.' He opened the car door, as he spoke. 'That he's innocent.'

'Isn't he?' I probed gently.

'In law . . . no.'

He ducked into the driver's seat and leaned over to unlatch the front passenger's door.

As I climbed into the car I said, 'You're copping out, Chris.'

'No.'

'Golders,' I said pointedly. 'He didn't kill *her*.'

'It doesn't prove much.' The engine turned sluggishly before it fired. 'Just that he didn't kill Golders.'

'Oh, for God's sake!'

'Okay.' He revved the engine, slipped the gear-stick into first, then moved the car away from the kerb. 'Let's find who *did* kill Golders. Then we'll lean. If he coughs Walters and Hewitt, that clears Turnbull.'

A thing which need not be mentioned. That four o'clock in the morning is a ridiculous time at which to arrive home. An evil hour; too late for bed, yet too early to start a new day. Added to which the house was cold: not the crisp, clean frostiness of the streets, but instead the chilling atmosphere of a series of lived-in rooms when the central heating has been off for a long time and the warmth has seeped its way through the lagging and double-glazing, leaving only a vague, sour, tomb-like legacy which will only clear with the opening of windows and the switching on of the radiators once more.

Mother and Aunt Elizabeth had long been in bed. I was alone with my thoughts . . . my unpleasant thoughts.

I flicked on the electric fire, then wandered into the kitchen to concoct myself a 'breakfast' of coffee and cold chicken and chutney sandwiches.

I carried the plate of sandwiches and the beaker of coffee back into the lounge, settled into an armchair, took off my shoes, loosened my tie, then started to eat. I suddenly discovered that I was hungry and, as a bonus, the act of eating alone at that unearthly hour carried with it a certain gentle – almost forbidden – enjoyment. For miles around people were sleeping, even the early-morning workers were still between the sheets. The world had yet to surface, had yet to discover the white rind of frost on outside surfaces, had yet to crawl, shivering, from the warmth of bedclothes and face a cold awakening.

And there was I. Comfortable. Munching tasty sandwiches. Sipping good coffee. Aware of so much which the rest of the world had to discover.

It was one of those odd episodes which punctuate every person's life. Unimportant in itself, yet for some mysterious reason, unforgettable. I knew that however long I lived – however many other meals I might enjoy – those sandwiches and that coffee consumed in the glow from the electric fire and sitting in the cushioned comfort of the armchair, would remain one meal I would always remember. I savoured it. Chewed slowly. Wallowed in the cosy ease of the chair. And wanted it to last forever.

A door opened behind me and Aunt Elizabeth's voice said, 'I *thought* I heard somebody moving around.'

I turned, smiled, and said, 'There's some coffee left. Want some?'

'Why not?' Her returned smile hinted at adventure.

'Sandwiches?'

'No, just coffee, please.'

I brought her coffee from the kitchen and she was curled up in the companion armchair to the one I'd vacated. Her slippered feet were tucked away out of sight. The slightly worn candlewick dressing-gown was pulled tight around her tiny body, and she looked remarkably like a lost child, just brought in from the cold.

'Cosy?' I asked.

She smiled and nodded as she took the proffered coffee.

Then for all of ten minutes we sat in silence. Warm. Happy. Content merely to be in each other's company.

I think everybody should have an Aunt Elizabeth; a maiden aunt whose simplicity and innocence does much to buffer the spikes of reality's harshness. They (it seems) know how to love. To *really* love. There is no qualification to their affection. They ask so little, but in return they give everlastingly. They don't ask to be admired. They don't ask to be respected. They don't even ask to be loved in return. All they ask is to be allowed to be *there*, and for that they happily pay a gentle, but outrageous, price.

With anybody else my previous contentment might have been shattered. With Aunt Elizabeth it was merely augmented and made more complete.

Quietly, timidly, as if afraid to break a spell, she said, 'You've had a long day, Eddie.'

I nodded.

'Those poor women,' she remarked and it was not an empty, something-to-say observation.

I said, 'They were loose women.'

'That's no reason,' she murmured.

There was more silence then, in little more than a whisper, she said, 'Sarah.'

'That name's not allowed, Aunt,' I reproved her gently.

'Your mother's fast asleep, Eddie. She can't hear it.'

'Nevertheless . . .'

Just the word. That's all I said. It came out as a sigh and was meaningless.

She asked, 'Don't you think of her sometimes?'

'Often,' I admitted softly.

'I remember . . .' Her eyes stared into the past and her voice was soft with good memories. 'I remember the first time I read her *Alice*. I think she liked *Through the Looking Glass* best. I think the topsy-turvy world fascinated her. I remember once seeing her staring into a mirror. I knew what she was thinking. Poor child.' She shook her head sadly, and repeated, 'Poor child,' as if it were a faint echo.

'She made her own choice,' I reminded her.

'No. Not quite.'

'Aunt, she . . .'

'She wanted to be different. That's all. Herself.'

'She was selfish. Father dead only a few weeks and . . .'

'She loved your father, Eddie.'

'I know.'

'I mean loved him. *Worshipped* him.'

'I know,' I repeated.

'You were always your mother's favourite. But with her . . .'

'I know,' I said wearily. 'Sarah was always father's child. And father died. And Sarah took it very badly. But's that's no reason for . . .'

'Ah, but it *is*, Eddie,' she insisted. 'To a woman – to

a young woman like Sarah – it's a very good reason indeed.'

I didn't argue. We were touching a forbidden subject. Had Mother been with us neither Aunt Elizabeth nor I would have dreamed of having such a discussion. A forbidden subject, therefore no room for argument.

I allowed the subject to sink into more silence.

But the mood was going. The comfortable, cosy, warm mood of companionship. It was melting away. It was gradually becoming sour.

On an impulse I said, 'Aunt . . .' Then I closed my mouth, amazed at my audacity.

'Yes?' she encouraged.

'Why . . .' I stumbled over the question, then said, 'Why didn't you ever get married?'

'Nobody ever asked me,' she said simply.

'Oh!'

'I'm glad.' She chuckled softly to herself. 'I've had the best of all worlds. Children . . . without the inconvenience of *having* children. A good home. The love of a good man – your father – but without carnality. I've been very fortunate.'

It was a point of view. One I hadn't previously thought of.

Then she threw the question back at me.

'Why haven't *you* ever got married, Eddie?'

'I don't know.' I tried to shrug the question off. 'Perhaps like you . . .'

'Oh, no.' She shook her head. 'Girls still wait to be asked.'

'Do they?' I smiled.

'The nice ones. The good ones.'

'Perhaps I haven't met any,' I fenced.

'Like Sarah?'

It was little more than a breath; less than a whisper in

that room of shadows and red glow. Something which should have remained unsaid, but which *was* said. Spoken so lightly, yet carrying so much heartbreak. She curled her fingers – the fingers of both hands – around her beaker, stared at me for a moment, then said, 'Christmas.'

'What about Christmas?' My voice was low and hoarse.

'Between us we could break down your mother's resistance.'

'No.'

'Sarah. Here for Christmas. Wouldn't you like that, Eddie?'

'No.'

'The nicest Christmas present of all.'

'No . . . it wouldn't be.'

'Eddie. Your own sister,' she pleaded.

'She left,' I groaned. 'Nobody sent her away.'

'You know better.'

'For God's sake . . .'

'Your mother forced her to leave. Both of them . . . your father's death played havoc with them both. Things were said. Things . . .'

'Sarah had a choice, Aunt Elizabeth. She chose to be selfish. To be hurtful. To go her own stupid way.'

'That's what your mother thinks, but . . .'

'That's what *I* think.'

'Eddie,' she pleaded sadly. 'All it needs is a word. It'll be Christmas. Christmas for Sarah, too, remember. A time for forgetting silly, petty squabbles. A time for . . .'

FIVE

Where was I? Ah yes, Aunt Elizabeth's pleading for Sarah.

It was wasted, of course. Poor Aunt Elizabeth. She tried so hard, but was unable to comprehend the depth of disgust felt by both Mother and I. Forgiving. Forgetting. The two words are not synonymous. Forgiving was out of the question. To forget was impossible. To forget meant never to remember . . . and to even *see* her would be to remember. Always!

Aunt Elizabeth returned to bed a little disappointed, I think. In order to ease the hurt of a flat refusal I'd promised to 'think it over', but I think she knew.

I drew the curtains, made fresh coffee and watched the dawn arrive. A cold, December dawn. Strangely different – strangely less invigorating – than the early hours of three and four o'clock. The mood had changed. My mood and with it the mood of the morning. The bitterness within my own mind was reflected by the bitterness of the outside world. Cold. Inhospitable. Brittle and unable to bend in response to arguments which to me had no validity.

I smoked cigarettes, sipped coffee and allowed the hands of the clock time in which to crawl their way into two more hours of daylight. Then I went upstairs, bathed, re-dressed, then (still taking my time) drove to Bowling Side Police Station and the Incident Centre.

A week passed. Or was it, perhaps, only six days? Or even eight? Without checking I can't be sure. Like the colours of cheap paint, caught in a downpour, each day ran into the next. There was no clear-cut demarkation line; there was nothing – no answer to any of the scores of questions we asked – which itemised any single day.

One thing I know for certain. That we interviewed and re-interviewed a veritable menagerie of vermin. The slimy Tomba Nayudu: we interrogated him twice in as many days; hard, threatening interrogations which almost had him weeping from frustration at his inability to convince us of his innocence. The whores and the men whom they kept – their so-called 'lovers'. The 'landladies' – the sluts who provided rooms and beds whenever some street woman required privacy in which to ply her trade.

And the decent people, too. They were in a minority but, even in a warren like Bowling Side, responsible and respectable citizens fight to retain their pride. They knew the area in which they lived. Some of them even knew the murdered women as neighbours or near-neighbours. But the few good people of Bowling Side rarely left their homes after dark. They 'minded their own business' with such single-mindedness as to make it almost a religion. This I understood. Even agreed with. But when good citizens who *want* to assist are helpless, the twilight people rarely do other than plead open-mouthed ignorance.

'They're bloody dumb,' raved Chris. 'We're here. We want to find the bastard responsible. We want to nail him. But – damnation – they won't even help.'

'Won't,' I agreed. 'Or can't.'

'The hell they can't! This whole festering area's a whispering gallery. They *know,* or if they don't know, they can make a damn good guess.'

'And if they guess wrong?' I asked quietly.

'We'll prove it, one way or the other.'

'Like we "proved" the case against Turnbull?'

'For Christ's sake, Eddie!'

'Chris.' We were in the car at the time and I reached

111

out a hand to stop him from turning the ignition key before I'd said what I wanted to say. I said, 'There's a tacit admission that we were wrong about Turnbull. This enquiry . . . it's a three-header. Walters, Hewitt and now Golders. That means something, Chris. For example. I don't know Turnbull's wife . . .'

'A nice woman. Tough enough not to wear her heart on her sleeve.'

'That's not what I mean. What I'm getting at is this. She must *know*. A third murder her husband couldn't possibly have committed . . .'

'Carbon copy.'

'My arse!' I said angrily. 'You don't believe that any more than I do. Any more than Lennox does. Or Harris, come to that. The carbon copy stunt always has something basically different. Something the original didn't have. These three come from the same stable . . . and you know it.'

'And?' His anger had been replaced by that weariness known only to policemen engaged on a major enquiry. The weariness of non-progress.

I said, 'Open the cell door. Give Turnbull his freedom.'

'Me? Personally?'

'Somebody,' I said heavily. 'The man's innocent. The hell with what the law says. The hell with what the court said. He's innocent.'

'So.' Chris turned the key and started the engine. 'Let's find the guilty bastard, that way we'll *prove* his innocence.'

But we didn't. We couldn't. The freemasonry of Bowling Side made damn sure of *that*. We enlarged the scope of our questioning. Instead of asking, 'Can you help us find the murderer of Elsie Golders?' and leaving it at that, we also asked, 'Can you help us prove that Turnbull didn't kill Emilia Walters or Bertha Hewitt?'. We wasted so much good breath. Nobody knew . . . and nobody *wanted* to know.

And yet . . .

With each passing day the silent, unbroken terror of Bowling Side grew. It grew as the uniformed patrols were removed to catch up with the back-log of normal police work. Bowling Side became haunted by a fear. The fear of the unknown; the fear of the unidentified; the fear that three might only be the beginning.

The street women still went about their business, but word reached us that Bowling Side had decided to organise counter-measures. Vigilante groups began to prowl the streets from about eleven o'clock until an hour or so before dawn. Hard men; some of them 'minders' of the women themselves and some of them bruisers paid by the less muscular pimps to ride herd upon their interests.

'It ain't on,' growled Lennox when word reached him of this latest development. 'No mob rule while I'm in charge o' the enquiry.'

'For what good *we're* doing . . .' Chris moved his shoulders. 'You can't really blame 'em.'

'Tallboy, old son,' said Lennox sombrely, 'those mad buggers don't represent the law. I hear some of 'em are armed. Pick-handles. Coshes. Christ knows what else. They find somebody, they clobber him, and what the hell happens if he's the wrong bloke?'

There was no answer to that question and Chris didn't try to invent one.

We were at the Incident Centre. We'd ended one more fruitless day of enquiries. It was past midnight and both Chris and I were tired. Lennox, too, looked as if a few days of solid sleep might not do him much harm. And for the umpteenth time we were talking the thing out.

Playing with ideas and opinions before we went home to bed.

Lennox mused, 'Somebody they all knew. Somebody who could stand in front of 'em, without arousing suspicion.'

'That seems to be the inference,' I agreed.

'Inference be damned.' Lennox's face screwed itself into a scowl. An unusual expression for this gross man; an expression which seemed to need a deliberate manipulation of the facial muscles. He said 'No sign of a struggle. Not a whisper. And these lasses aren't vicarage tea party types. One o' the first things they learn is how to handle an awkward customer.'

'Talking to somebody,' suggested Chris.

'Talking. Chatting. Passing the time o' day. Somebody they knew.'

'A potential client?' I suggested.

'Possibly.' Lennox didn't sound too sure. 'A client each woman knew, though. Knew. Trusted. Didn't suspect. Aye – a client – possibly, but that's a long shot. Somebody Walters, Hewitt and Golders all knew well. Somebody like that, though y'know they'd know the name. Talk. Somebody in Bowling Side would know the name of the bloke who favoured those three. We'd have heard.'

'They're like bloody oysters,' I murmured.

Chris said, 'Okay. Somebody standing in front of 'em. Relaxed and friendly. Then a grab for the throat, no time to struggle, no time to scream, no time for *anything*, somebody with muscle. Eh?'

'I've had a word with the experts,' rumbled Lennox. 'The boffins tell me things. Muscle ain't necessary. Just to know the right place to squeeze, and this one *did* know. Seconds. That's all. Cut the blood supply to the brain. She's unconscious in seconds, before she's got over the initial shock. Then just keep squeezing.'

114

Chris breathed, 'Christ!'

'Technical,' I observed.

'Basic,' rumbled Lennox. 'A doctor. A medical student. A good first aid man.' He paused, then added, 'A nurse.'

'A nurse?' Chris blinked. 'Y'mean . . .'

'The female o' the species, old cock.' Lennox tried to force a grin across his tired face. 'We've tried everything. Let's try skirts for a change. It's at least *possible*.'

Chris said, 'Women don't strangle,' but the remark carried little conviction.

'Not often,' agreed Lennox. 'But, y'know, it ain't impossible.'

'And the motive?' asked Chris.

'Lookee . . .' Lennox passed the palms of his hands from front to back across his bald pate. For a moment he looked his age . . . and more. For a moment the weight of responsibility showed in the puzzled sadness of his eyes. He said, 'Murder. Who the hell knows the motive? Ever? We shove a so-called "motive" on the plate and show it to the jury, but we don't *know*. Nobody knows. This lot – maybe some poor sod's caught a packet from the Walters woman. Maybe he's taking it out on all the other Bowling Side bags. Maybe Turnbull *did* do the Walters woman – V.D. or because she was in the club – then killed the Hewitt woman as a cover-up. Maybe the Golders killing *was* a carbon copy, after all. Or, if you like, the Walters strangling, then the other *two* carbon copies. Drag carbon copies into things and you have *two* motives, and that screws things up very nicely. Call it a woman. For the sake of argument, let's say we're after a woman. Okay, why should a woman kill a woman? Why should a woman kill *three* women? What sort of a motive can a woman have for killing three whores? Because *she's* a whore? Because she's jealous? Because she's *not* a whore? Because she has a hatred of whores?

Whores generally? Or whores specifically? And if specifically just these three? And if not just these three how many more? And if it's a general hatred, again how many more?'

'It becomes involved,' observed Chris gently.

'Tallboy, old son, it's *always* involved.' Lennox sighed. 'The mind . . . see? Murder. It's a thing o' the mind. A mental state. Our job's to fart around till we get something a bit more substantial than the mind. Something we can explain in English primer language. Something every dumb bastard on the jury can understand. Something they can feel, something they can see, something they can smell. Something some stupid bloody judge can yammer on about. After that who gives a toss about the motive? We come up with a *reason*. That's all. Not a motive. I press that switch . . .' He nodded towards the door of the Incident Centre. 'The light goes out. That's the *reason*, because I pressed the switch. But that's all balls. The *real* reason is because I've cut off the electricity, but who the hell can explain what electricity is? Electricity. That's the motive power . . . see? The "motive" if you like. The switch is only the reason. Okay, in court we trot out the reason – the switch that turns the juice on or off. But we're allowed to call it "motive" because we can't explain and nobody would understand the "electricity". Hell's bells!' He suddenly seemed to explode into a burst of frustrated anger. ' "That cat sat on the mat" . . . great. Now what sort o' cat was it? And what sort o' mat? And when you've decided *that*, start explaining it all to a blind man. That's the crackpot jury system we're all so flaming proud of. Twelve people. Probably never seen the inside of a court in their life. And *they're* going to have to listen to mumbo-jumbo they don't understand and, at the end of it all, decide

whether this man or this woman committed murder . . .
and why. Babes and bloody sucklings!'

He closed his mouth and the glint of anger left his
eyes. It was as if he'd remembered the role he was expected to play. The fat man incapable of taking anything
too seriously, the grown-up Billy Bunter who just *happened* to be a detective chief superintendent.

'Sorry.' His grin was a little shamefaced. 'It's just,
y'know, the law. Inadequate. Clumsy sometimes. This
damn enquiry. It seems to be getting bogged down. And
. . . ' He pushed himself upright. 'I'm a little short on
sleep. We all are. See you both tomorrow. Who knows?
We might suddenly crack the bloody thing.'

We didn't, that goes without saying. I knew we wouldn't.

But I also knew something else.

I stayed behind after both Lennox and Chris had left for
home. I sat at a corner table and idly played the cassettes
on to which various witnesses had recorded their statements to be typed out the next day when the clerks and
typists came on duty. I sat there and pondered upon
Lennox's outburst.

So true. So bloody *true*! He'd touched gold; I doubt if
he'd realised it, but he'd touched pure gold.

The average – the everyman's – idea concerning a murder
enquiry. So wrong. So ridiculous. Spawned, no doubt, by
the cinema and television screens. But if so, augmented by
newsreel interviews given by senior police officers, who
mouth carefully considered platitudes in answer to questions which are no questions at all.

(Harris, if you recall, was so interviewed a couple of
times. He sounded so certain. The impression given was
that we already *knew* – that *he* already knew – that given

a few more days sufficient evidence would be available to make an arrest.)

I tell you . . .

The murder enquiry without a lead – without an immediate lead – is little more than a glorified guessing game. Put crudely, the shit is thrown at the spinning blades of the fan in the hope that some of it will stick on the guilty party.

The fan was Bowling Side and Chris and I were doing more than our fair share of throwing.

During that latter half of December we'd been reduced to virtually accusing everybody and anybody.

'He's not necessarily from this district,' I protested.

'He . . . or she,' muttered Chris.

'But not necessarily from Bowling Side.'

'Okay. Not necessarily from Kemington. Not necessarily from Bordfield. But what the hell else do we do?'

Our tempers were fraying, badly. And with cause. The Bowling Siders were demanding positive action and who could blame them? Their own vigilante groups prowled the streets and, on at least three occasions, terrified innocent men seeking copulatory excitement. More than once we warned such groups of the illegality of mob rule.

'Get the hell off the streets.' Chris, like myself, was in no mood for police conversation.

'Get stuffed!' The brawler with the ripping-bar held tight in his right fist met fury with fury. 'You pansy-faced gits can't find the bleeder. But *we* will.'

'That thing.' Chris nodded at the ripping-bar.

'What about it?'

'You thinking of using it?'

'What do *you* think?'

'You're a bloody fool.'

'*He* won't think so.'

I snarled, 'Take the damn thing home. And the rest of

you . . . clear the street. Or I'll have you all wanged inside for unlawful assembly.'

'Hey, Caan.' I recognised the second speaker as a part-time-pimp I'd crossed swords with in the past. 'You ain't talking to birds hawking their pussy this time. We'll bloody soon . . .'

'Shurrup!' The man with the ripping-bar was the leader. He said, 'Okay, Mr Tallboy. We'll move, but we'll get together again the minute you're clear. We're gonna find him. See? And when we've found him, we'll give you a ring. Tell you which alley to go to.'

When we'd left them Chris growled, 'Who can blame 'em?'

'Three unimportant harlots,' I sneered. 'Alive any one of that crowd would have smacked any of them in the teeth for saying a word out of place. Dead they're bloody nigh saints.'

'Three women. Three human beings.' Chris stopped and voiced a concern which, although I understood it, I did not share. He said, 'Eddie, this place is on a short fuse. We'd better find him whoever he is, because if we *don't* . . .'

The tension grew and the animals of Bowling Side became more restless. Like a zoo (far more like a zoo than a jungle because the animals were trapped in their respective cages) and like when one of the cats scents unseen danger. The reaction was identical. They prowled their tiny territory. They spat and snarled with undue savagery. They were aware of their own final helplessness, and that in itself increased their fury and their eagerness to maim whoever they suspected of being the cause of their terror.

A den of animals, then. And because pressure of duty had depleted the original force thrown into the district when Golders had been found strangled Chris and I walked the den, day after day, night after night.

Our presence helped to keep the animals subdued . . . a little. Like trainers, we drove them back into their allocated cages. And gradually – as if by tacit approval – our fruitless enquiries enveloped *three* murders . . . not one.

Christmas arrived.

Christmas!

I can tell it now. Never, since father's death, have I enjoyed Christmas. Not once. Christmas: the time of joy; the time of good food and good drink; the time of present-giving. But not for us . . . *never* for us. Ours was not a Dickensian Christmas. It was not a religious Christmas. Damnation, it wasn't even a pleasant Christmas. It was a time of mourning; a time of death rather than a time of birth. Christmas Day was a sombre, hateful day. Filled with great, sad silences. Haunted by the tight-lipped, hard-eyed expression with which mother killed any hope of laughter.

I worked that Christmas Day morning. I worked until well past midday. I wore uniform for the first time in weeks; patrolled the streets of Bowling Side in my car, exchanged greetings with the few constables on duty and watched the Bowling Siders make ready for the boozing, shouting, laughing, fighting Bedlam of the coming evening and night.

At the police station I issued the usual instructions to the sergeant in charge.

'Pass the word, sergeant. The fewer people in the cells tonight, the better.'

'Yes sir.'

'Point the drunks for home, then leave 'em.'

'I'll see the word gets round, sir.'

'Anything short of a riot, let them fight each other into the ground.'

'The usual relaxation.' The sergeant grinned.

'Controlled relaxation, Sergeant. So far . . . no farther.'

'Leave it to me, sir.'

I said, 'I'll be at home. If things get out of hand give me a ring.'

'Yes, sir.' As I turned to go he added, 'Compliments of the season, sir.'

'Eh?'

'A merry Christmas, if it isn't too late.'

'Oh! Same to you, sergeant. Same to you.'

But I knew, it wasn't going to be a 'merry' Christmas. It hadn't been a 'merry' Christmas for years. As always it was going to be a very miserable Christmas.

It was, too. If anything, more miserable than ever.

Poor, dear Aunt Elizabeth. She'd tried to make it a little 'traditional'. She'd incurred Mother's displeasure by placing tiny sprigs of holly behind some of the photographs hanging on the wall of the lounge and, above the fireplace, she'd strung a pathetic little paper-chain. A home-made paper-chain, like the ones made by Christmas bound patients when, years ago, she'd worked at the local hospital. Not gaudy. Not even particularly well made. Just a touch, a hint, of what the day supposedly represented.

As I walked into the lounge, Mother was saying, 'Take them down, Elizabeth.'

'But, Hannah, they're so . . .'

'Take them down immediately.'

As I closed the door I said, 'No. Leave them up, Aunt Elizabeth.'

'Edmund . . .'

'Mother.' I smiled, walked to a chair and sat down. 'Such a small thing. A paper-chain. A few sprigs of holly. Don't let's bicker today of all days.'

'If they stay up . . .'

'They're staying up, Mother. You're the elder of the house, but I'm the head. Since father died I've accepted that responsibility. It also means I make decisions.'

'Eddie.' Aunt Elizabeth was caught between our difference of opinion. She looked unhappy. Embarrassed. She said, 'If your mother insists . . .'

'I insist.'

'Oh!'

'I'm going to my room,' snapped Mother.

'As you wish.' I nodded. 'One of us will call you when dinner's ready.'

'I don't want dinner. I don't *need* dinner.'

'Mother!' I saw no reason to keep the irritation from my tone. 'If you see fit to behave like a spoiled child, that's your prerogative. But there'll be a place laid. And you'll be told. Be assured, eventually hunger will drive you to the table.'

'I'll – I'll bring you your meal up,' stammered Aunt Elizabeth.

I snapped, 'No. The hell she will. You'll come down and eat like a civilised human being.'

It was (need I say?) a most miserable Christmas Day. Some cheap coloured paper. A few twigs of holly. Was there ever less reason for a family squabble?

Mother was stubborn. But so was I. Our respective obstinacies clashed and neither of us saw reason to apologise. She, I knew, was using Christmas as a 'Remembrance Day'; as a marker for the time when our family was shattered, never quite to recover. It was stupid and I saw no good reason for it. Whatever the past, the present was *now* and looking over our shoulders with angry, heartbroken eyes was neither sane nor healthy.

Damnation the rest of the world was celebrating. We, it would seem, were mourning and, moreover, would continue to mourn for the rest of our lives. Or (to be accurate) would so continue, if mother had her way.

We ate our meal in silence; a silence which throughout that afternoon had hardly been broken. Then as we sipped coffee and as I smoked a cigarette, Aunt Elizabeth tentatively tried to mend the breach.

'Eddie,' she murmured, 'she's a sick woman.'

'What's her disease?' I asked harshly.

'You know. I don't have to . . .'

'Psychosomatic,' I interrupted bluntly. 'The doctors – the specialists – there's damn-all wrong with her. She's hungry for sympathy. If she's ill she'll *get* sympathy, so she's ill.'

'It's not a feigned illness, Eddie.'

'Self-induced,' I growled, 'which means the same thing.'

'No.' Aunt Elizabeth shook her head.

'She . . .' I hesitated, then decided to voice the truth. 'She pins us down. You. Me. She has this un-named, unknown ailment and she *uses* it. And we're fools enough to let her.'

'Eddie!'

'No.' I brushed her protestations aside. 'We've made enough excuses. Mother this. Mother that. Mother the other. She's as fit as you are. She was shocked when it happened, okay, she was shocked. *I* was shocked. *You* were shocked. But – the hell! – we didn't crawl into a hole and expect the world to play lackey to us. Father died. Okay, people *do* die. Everybody. All the flags in the world don't have to fly at half-mast for the rest of creation. *That's* the illness. That's the only illness. And – dammit – we've pandered to the stupidity too long.'

'Not just your father,' she murmured gently.

'All right.' I felt the rage rising inside me. 'Sarah, she died too. If necessary, let's say two people died. Two

123

people ceased to exist. Three of us are still here . . . and we're *not* dead.'

'Do you really believe that, Eddie?'

'We're not dead,' I muttered savagely.

'Dear, sweet Eddie.' There was a depth of affection which surprised me. 'You have so little fun out of life. So little enjoyment.'

'I get along,' I growled.

'But that's not living . . . is it?'

'It's all I ask. Without Mother's tantrums, it's all I want.'

'I wonder. I really wonder.'

I, too, wondered. That was the truth of the matter. I wondered if I was deluding myself and, if so, for how long. Whether this self-delusion – assuming it to be there – had become so much a part of me that by this time I was incapable of recognising it.

I was, I knew, unable to enthuse about anything. By and large my emotions remained on a plateau of equinimity: I had neither wild peaks of ecstasy nor dark troughs of despair. Over the years I had schooled myself to control my feelings. To remain outwardly calm and unmoved. To remain inwardly uninvolved.

But (and this was the rub) I'd *schooled* myself.

One can do this. Given the desire it is possible, even easy, to take objectivity and make of it a near-religion. The result is a robot-like existence. The arts – fine music, great paintings, superb acting, magnificent writing – are all appreciated and applauded. But a lump never comes to the throat. A tear never threatens to spill from the eye. The nape hairs never tingle. Art, it seems, is removed from its true world and, via this objectivity, demoted into the sphere of craftsmanship. Genius is denied . . . only exceptional talent is acknowledged.

Which (as I pondered the problem) posed the obvious question.

Had I always been so 'uninvolved'? Had there perhaps been a time long forgotten when, say, a Schubert symphony might have raised me high enough to speak with angels? Somewhere in my life were there unremembered years when fine prose or poetry had touched hidden springs of incandescent joy or sadness? Or had I since birth carried this awful vacuum? This inbuilt arrogance which, as far as I was concerned, denied the existence of beauty beyond description? This void which refused me a full life?

It worried me. Indeed, the possibility enraged me.

Aunt Elizabeth entered the lounge, where I was sitting with my thoughts, and said, 'The television, dear? The Christmas programmes are just about to begin.'

'No.'

In my present mood I wanted no *ersatz* snow, no prancing chorus girls with festive dance routines, no Christmas comedians with their tired up-dated patter. What I wanted was . . .

Reassurance, perhaps? Somebody – somebody whom I trusted and believed – who might convince me that I was not 'different'.

Aunt Elizabeth read my eyes and said, 'Eddie. There's something troubling you.'

'Something,' I admitted.

'If it's about your mother . . .'

'Damn Mother!'

'Oh!' She frowned at the impatient anger of my tone, lowered herself into a chair and said, 'Can I help?'

'I doubt it.'

'I can try,' she encouraged.

I hesitated, then said, 'All right.' I took a deep breath,

tried to spear the truth and said, 'All right, first question : why don't I laugh?'

'I – I beg your pardon?' She looked shocked.

'Laugh,' I said harshly. 'Other men laugh. Other men are touched by humour. Come to that, other men are touched by tragedy. They cry, or want to cry, so why not *me*?'

'Eddie, dear, you're not making too much sense.'

'When did you last hear me laugh?' I asked.

'Why – er – you often . . .'

'No.' I shook my head. 'Not smile. Not smirk politely because it was expected of me. *Laugh*! Feel genuine enjoyment? Chuckle? know the meaning of spontaneous humour? Laugh, dammit, laugh? I can't remember. Can you?'

'No.' She spoke slowly. 'You want the truth. I can't remember when I last heard you laugh.'

'As a child?' I asked.

She gave a fleeting smile and said, 'Yes, you were a happy child. You laughed a great deal then. You laughed long before you could talk.'

'Therefore?'

'I – I don't know what you want me to say, Eddie. I – I suppose a man grows up as his environment allows him. You're a police officer. Your work allows little scope for amusement.'

'No, you're wrong.' I shook my head. 'I know happy policemen. Most policemen are happy. The canteen chatter, for example. Jokes are the order of the day. Laughter. You never heard such laughter than when policemen get together.'

'This enquiry, then,' she suggested. 'You've taken it very much to heart, or so it seems.'

'Perhaps,' I admitted.

'Obviously.' She pursued what she thought was the

cause of my worry. 'Three women – young women – all murdered. All strangled. All . . .'

'Three alley cats,' I interrupted gently, but grimly. 'That's all they are. That's all they were. Tragedy too, you see. No feeling. No compassion.'

'But you *have* taken it to heart,' she insisted.

'Turnbull,' I said.

'The constable who was convicted of the first two murders?'

'He was innocent.'

'How can you be so sure?' The question carried worry and concern.

'Aunt Elizabeth.' I sighed. 'The third killing. The Golders woman. He *can't* have strangled her. But the same man – the same person – was responsible for all three crimes. It's illogical – ridiculous – to argue otherwise.'

'The same – er – person? You mean not necessarily a man?'

'That's Chief Superintendent Lennox's idea.'

'Oh!'

There was a gap in our conversation. Like all such conversations we'd started on one topic and, without realising it, moved on to another. Questions had been asked, but had not been answered. The original cause of my black mood remained.

A little wrily I murmured, 'But still no laughter.'

'Is it so important?'

'Incapable of any depth of emotion. Incapable of love.'

'Oh, come now, Eddie,' she protested. 'You love me. You love your mother.'

'No!' It was a time for truth. Time for tearing away the façade of pretence. Time, if necessary, to hurt. Very deliberately I said, 'I like you, Aunt Elizabeth. I admire you. You are – as you must know – a person with whom nobody could be angry. An innocent. A child. If you left, I'd miss you. I'd be sorry. But I wouldn't be heart-broken. The fault is with me, not you. God knows you deserve to be loved. What you've done for me. The burden you've accepted without complaint since father died. You *deserve* it. But I have none . . .' I moved my hands help-lessly. 'But I have none. I can't give what I don't possess.'

'Your – your mother,' she said softly. 'Surely . . .'

'With her it's a duty. A tiresome duty. I've been taught. Trained. Brainwashed. But that's not love. She gave me life . . . something I didn't ask for. As a child she fed me, clothed me, housed me, but that was *her* duty. She, too, had been brainwashed. But that's not love. Neither from me, nor from her. Look at her . . .' Again I moved my hands. 'Not as a sister, not as a son. Look at her as a woman. As Hannah Caan. What do you see? I'll tell you what *I* see. An embittered, selfish, unforgiving woman. Sick? Oh yes sick, by reason of her own monumental self-pity. Mentally sick and wallowing in it. Enjoying it. Love her? *Her*?' The bile threatened to choke me. 'The last person on God's earth. The last person on God's earth deserving of love. The truth is I love nobody, Aunt Eliza-beth. It's something I'm incapable of. Something I can't do. Like laughter. *I can't love.*'

Untrue of course. I had loved. Perhaps I still loved, but certainly I *had* loved. And been loved in return.

Sarah. My laughing, delightful Sarah. I would argue that the love of a brother for his sister – and indeed the love of a sister for her brother – is strangely unique. It doesn't always happen, but when it does it is magnificent and splendid.

Men, I know, love their wives. And this, too, is a great and all-enveloping love. But no greater than the brother-sister love. Different, perhaps, but no greater.

For years Sarah was my lady. Every day I rode out to her rescue. Every day I was her knight and every day she was my maiden in distress. The bond was complete. Absolute. And – or so it seemed – indestructible. I was a quiet child, something of an introvert. She, on the other hand, had a touch of tomboy in her. The two things made us perfect equals. She could run as fast as I. She could climb any tree I could climb. She could, when occasion demanded, fight like an enraged tigress . . . as angrily and as effectively as I.

But we never fought each other. To have done so – to have even argued – would have been a blasphemy. No, when we fought – the few times we did fight – we fought side by side and against the world.

In my eyes she could do no wrong. In her eyes I was equally immaculate.

And then . . .

Ah, yes . . . but we don't talk about it, do we? Sarah's name is forbidden. The very thought of Sarah is discouraged.

And yet with her I could laugh. With her I knew the meaning of love. With her I was complete.

My beloved Sarah . . .

Those half-dozen days which link Christmas with New Year are the ridiculous days of the calender. They are the Old Year passing into history with boorish buffoonery. They are neither one thing nor the other; neither working days nor holidays. At best they are a pause in which to sober up prior to another orgy of drunkenness; a time in which to let the stomach settle before another bout of indigestion.

In the force they were and still are a respite when those who were on duty at Christmas can, perhaps, take time off in lieu before New Year's Eve arrives, and with it *more* extra duty.

For myself I was uninterested. Chris – a family man with stronger feelings towards this season than I – was on holiday until January 3rd. It seemed sensible therefore that I should revert back to uniformed duty for a few days and thus help ease the pressure on the non-C.I.D. branch at this most ludicrous time of the year.

Not that the murder enquiry would miss my presence.

As with Walters and Hewitt the initial impetus following the Golders killing had slowed down considerably.

This seasonal lethargy was as always felt in the force, too. The pre-Christmas increase in fowl-thieving and shop-lifting had eased. The upsurge of car thefts, drunken driving and general booze-induced lunacy had quietened until the New Year. The yearly, bleary-eyed period of near-normality – the pause before the second wind of rowdyism – was with us.

It was there when I walked into the Incident Centre at about eight o'clock that last evening of the old year.

Lennox was there. Nobody else. The fat man was smoking a large and very obviously cheap cigar, at a guess one of the last of his Christmas presents. He was staring, through a haze of smoke, at the three opened files on the trestle-table desk. His concentration was absolute and he was unaware of my presence until I was well into the room.

Then he raised his head and said, 'Ah, Caan, old cock.'

'Sir.' (Odd. One tends to use that particular noun more readily when in uniform.)

'Out on the street?' he asked.

'Keeping the rabble quiet,' I agreed.

He grunted, removed the cigar from his mouth, waved it at the open files, then said, 'This lot. We'll need to do summat about it once we get back into gear.'

'The murders?'

'Three of 'em.'

Straight-faced I said, 'But two detected . . . surely?'

His eyes narrowed slightly and he growled, 'Don't be sarcy, old son.'

'They *are* detected, sir,' I insisted.

'Just occasionally . . .' He drew on the cigar, then continued, 'Just now and again we make a mistake. We ain't perfect.' The cigar, the figure, the manner in which he sat hunched over the table, even the low growl of his voice reminded me vividly of Churchill in one of his more bloody-minded moods. He said, 'The crime ain't in making the mistake, son. The crime's in not *admitting* the mistake. We dropped a clanger with Turnbull . . . who the hell else says otherwise, I'm convinced o' that.'

'In that case . . .'

'Unfortunately,' he continued as if I hadn't spoken, 'the law doesn't move into reverse too easily. Appeals to Home Secretaries – all that crap – it takes months, years. And even then you might end up with a horse laugh. Home Secretaries don't like to think their lovely jury system sometimes comes off the rails. So . . .' He jerked his head up and looked at my face. 'What d'we do, son? What suggestions have you in mind?'

'Find the right man,' I said.

'Or woman.'

'Or woman,' I agreed.

'Sit down.' He waved the cigar. 'Let's see how we make out. Three jigsaw puzzles. Let's push 'em around a bit. See which pieces fit all three.'

I removed my peak cap and lowered myself into a handy chair.

'Right.' He touched the files with a thick forefinger. 'Let's see what they have in common first. Get that out o' the way. Three women.'

'Three prostitutes,' I contributed.

'Right.' He nodded.

'All from Bowling Side. All with previous convictions.'

'Right.' He continued to nod agreement, then said, 'But one in the family way, the other two not.'

'One diseased, the other two not,' I contributed.

He mused, 'The age group ain't much help, either. Too broad a span. Not dolly birds. Not old bags. Somewhere inbetween, and that covers too much ground to be much of a lead.'

'Two of them shared the same living quarters,' I suggested.

'True, but the third lived alone.'

'They all used Henry's eating-place.'

'They *all* use Henry's eating place,' he countered. 'It might be interesting if one of 'em hadn't.'

I said, 'All right, sir. Basics. They were all strangled.'

'Now we're moving.' Again he nodded. 'That means no weapons. No blunt instruments. No guns, no knives. Important, eh?'

'Possibly,' I agreed.

'Strangled, then hidden.'

I nodded.

'But,' he added, '*not* hidden.'

'Sir?'

'The shoe. The coat. The glove.'

'Oh! I see.'

'Aye.' He scowled. 'And *he* wanted us to "see", or *she* wanted us to "see".'

'Quite,' I agreed.

'Like a bloody arrow. Pointing. "X marks the spot". That's the bit I find interesting.'

'Unusual.'

'Bloody barmy,' he said bluntly. 'Unless there's a reason.'

'At the very least – er – fascinating,' I murmured.

'Barmy,' he insisted. He paused then added, 'Unless you link it in with the other thing.'

'What other thing?'

'Three bodies . . . all found by coppers. Turnbull. Hobson. Yourself. Warlock. *Then* this "X marks the spot" codswallop starts to make sense, of a sort.'

'I'm sorry, sir. I don't . . .'

'He wanted 'em found. Or *she* wanted 'em found. More than that – found by one of us. That's my reading. What d'you make of it, Caan, old son?'

I thought for a moment, then said, 'He, or she, was cutting it very fine – if you're right.'

'Assume I'm right,' he suggested.

'To see an officer coming – to see one approaching – *then* to do the killing. That's taking one hell of a risk.'

'Ain't it, though?' He grinned.

I nodded and wondered what the devil he was *really* thinking.

Without warning he switched subjects and asked, 'Paid your respects to Mrs Turnbull this Christmas, son?'

'Eh – er, no. No. It never entered my head to visit . . .'

'She's taking it hard.' His expression was sad. His voice was quiet and sombre. 'I called in. She's bitter.'

'Who can blame her?'

'True.' He sighed. 'A rum bloke, Turnbull.'

'Rum?'

'Queer. Some of 'em are never satisfied. They don't know their own luck till it's too late.'

'I – I didn't know him that well.'

'Nice lass.' He seemed to be talking to himself. 'Neat little house. Thinks the world of him. *Still* thinks the world of him, despite his fannying around with the Walters woman. It takes a good wife to do that.'

'Yes, I suppose so.'

'And now . . .' He moved his hands. 'Her whole world gone. Like us, she's sure he's innocent. *Knows* he's innocent – woman's intuition or summat. The bastard who *did* do the killing should be made to visit her. See for himself.'

'I doubt if it would do much good,' I muttered.

'Oh, I dunno.' A sad grin touched his lips. 'Worth a try if we could find him.'

'If we could find him,' I echoed.

He stretched his arms and said, 'Well, I'm for home. The missus likes us to see the New Year in together if possible. Pity the Turnbulls can't.'

I stood up, replaced my peaked cap and made to leave the Incident Centre.

As I reached the door he said, 'Give it some thought, eh? Some reason for a copper always finding the body.'

A strange night. For a New Year's Eve a most peculiar night. Without stars, without moon and with a thick low blanket of cloud which seemed to have a suffocating effect. Nor did the vagaries of the English climate help matters; from the keen frosts of a few nights before some oddity of meteorological absurdity had brought in a night as warm as that of summer, but without the bonus of even a slight breeze.

I parked the car and strolled the streets of Bowling Side.

The darkness of smashed street-lighting seemed to add to the unseasonal heat. I felt the stickiness of perspiration cling my clothes to my skin and breathing was a conscious effort.

Like . . .

Those summers of many years ago. Meadow grass and the shallow, stone-chuckling river. A blue dome with sometimes as many as three skylarks scattering their confetti-like songs as they climbed out of sight. And two children busy threading daisy-chains. The drone of insects and the gentle snore of father as he napped with a spread handkerchief covering his face. And mother . . . mildly critical of everything. Of *everything*!

For the evening it was quiet. As yet the rowdyism was a thing of the future. The public houses, though open and catering for early custom, were still poised for the explosion of roaring, fighting vandalism with which the coming year would be greeted. But for now the streets were almost deserted. The occasional click of high heels hurrying along a pavement, the steadier and louder slap of heavier shoes . . . and in the darkness always the sound before the sight.

And the feeling. Almost a physical thing. The fear of the unknown. The unidentified. It had become part of Bowling Side itself. Part of the ever-present stench. Part of the threatening mystery with which the district greeted all strangers. But this time the Bowling Siders also felt the threat. Something – somebody – was threatening *them*. And like the ignorants they were, they were afraid of the unknown.

Like . . .

That deep, rectangular hole in the earth. The wet earth and the ceaseless drizzle which soaked everybody and brought an extra sheen to the lid of the coffin. And the piled up clay of the soil with slippery planks across its top. And the mourners filing slowly past the hole. Staring down. Curious, but not really saddened. Reading the silver name-plate, but without it meaning anything.

And two people to whom it *did* mean something talking in whispers, away from the sombrely dressed rubber-neckers.

'I'm leaving, Eddie.'

'What?'

'Leaving. Leaving home.'

'For God's sake, Sarah. What are you saying? You *cant*.'

'Without Father, I can't stand Mother.'

'Look . . . Oh, for heaven's sake, Sarah! You don't *mean* it.'

'She's impossible.'

'She's – she's difficult. But . . . She'll . . .'

'She'll get worse.'

'You don't know that. Give her a chance. At least . . .'

'No. It has to be now, Eddie. Now! Otherwise it'll be too late.'

'Sarah, for God's sake!'

'Aunt Elizabeth will move in with you.'

'I don't want Aunt Elizabeth. I want *you*. We've been – we've been . . .'

'I know, Eddie, darling. We've been so close. You, me, Father. Together we could fight her. Three of us. But just the two of us. We're not strong enough. She'll . . .'

SIX

It doesn't matter. What you've missed – what isn't on the other side doesn't matter – you'll dig and find out, and anyway it has little to do with what I'm telling you.

That night. That New Year's Eve. It was I suppose a time of ghosts. A time of hauntings. I walked those foul streets and was haunted – haunted by phantoms of living people. Sarah. Turnbull. Mrs Turnbull. Strange that . . . wouldn't you agree? That the ghosts of people still alive can haunt?

Nevertheless, you have my word. They are, perhaps, the only *real* ghosts. The only *genuine* spectres capable of crowding in and playing havoc with the cosy, comfortable world of reality.

And Lennox, of course. A very fat ghost. A very substantial ghost. But I think the most threatening ghost of all. The others could be rendered harmless; they could – with some great effort – be brushed aside and ignored. Even Sarah. Even Turnbull. But not Lennox, because Lennox had worked his way inside me; was part of me and, whilever *he* was there, the others had a resting place.

Sarah. Where *was* Sarah? How was *she* spending this New Year's Eve?

There'd been rumours. Whisperings a few years back. That she'd made a somewhat belated effort to become an actress of some sort. Nothing great. No overnight super-star. Assistant stage manager at some tottering repertory theatre in the Midlands. A few non-speaking parts, perhaps. Then, with luck, a line or two. The so-called 'live' theatre at its lowest level.

I knew what *that* meant.

A form of conversation bespattered with meaningless endearments. Creatures who lived as big a lie off the stage as they did on. A profession (profession!) riddled with graft and perversion. A life in which homosexuality and promiscuity was accepted as a twisted norm.

The sweat almost squirted from my pores but it was not the heat of the night which saturated my shirt and caused rivulets of perspiration to run down my face.

Sarah. *My* Sarah! In some filthy, flea-ridden theatrical digs. Trading her body – marketing her innocence – for *that*.

At this time of the year in some cheap and tatty pantomime. In my mind's eye I could see her, cavorting across some dingy stage, illuminated by the glare of theatrical lighting. Dressed in barely concealing tights. As near as dammit exposing herself to the drooling males of the audience.

The thought. The vision. The *possibility*!

I muttered, 'Damn you. Damn you, Sarah, for destroying something beautiful. For not staying with me. For not understanding. For not *knowing* that, whilever I was there, Mother couldn't hurt you. For weakening me and making me what I am. Damn you to hell.'

But, God help me, I didn't mean it. I couldn't mean it.

And the second ghost. The ghost of Turnbull.

Such a pathetic ghost. The ghost who shouldn't have been a ghost. The man who, because of his own carnality, was now buried behind the walls of a prison.

What sort of a Christmas? What sort of a New Year? What sort of a life. A terrible thought – that although many men serving prison sentences claim innocence, some truly *are* innocent. Turnbull, for example. What were his thoughts when he was charged? What were his

138

thoughts when he heard the jury's verdict? When he heard the judge's sentence?

A world turned upside down and inside out. A world where innocence was punished and guilt remained free. What *are* a man's thoughts when he finds himself an inmate of such a world? Bitterness? One hell of a bitterness, that for sure. But what else? Like an animal caught in an escape-proof trap, therefore almost homicidal panic. And more than that. A knowledge : a knowledge that stays with him every minute, every hour, every day, that one other person knows the certainty of his innocence. One other person knows. Doesn't merely 'believe'. Knows!

The shade of Turnbull haunted me that night as I walked the dark streets of Bowling Side and once more I mumbled promises to myself . . . and to him.

'I'll get you out, Turnbull. Whatever the cost I'll *make* them believe. Trust me. It can be done. It's already been done, it can be done again. And if necessary again. And again and again . . . until they *have* to accept their error.'

But he haunted me still. And his wife. They refused to leave me. They denied me peace.

Dear God, his wife!

An unknown woman. Lennox had said she was a good woman and I had no reason to doubt the assessment. A good woman, a ghost without a face. The most broken-hearted ghost of all. Did she believe? I don't mean did she pretend belief for the sake of her own sanity, for the sake of her husband's sanity. I mean did she *believe*?

How the hell could she? How the hell could she be one hundred per cent sure? A copper's wife. She believed in the law for years, she'd lived with a belief in the law. Her husband had represented – *still* represented – the infallibility of that law. So how the hell *could* she believe?

Innocent? Despite what the law said?

One corner of her mind *had* to insist that she was the

wife of a murderer. The alternative was to deny every-thing her husband had stood for. Could any woman make such a denial? Do such an about-face? Accept such a monumental lie in the face of evidence to the contrary?

She, too, haunted me in the black streets of Bowling Side. Another ghost. Without face, without shape, but with a real presence.

Ah, but the most fearsome ghost of all. Lennox. The taunting ghost. The mocking ghost. The ghost who knew the truth – knew that *I* knew the truth – and knew that *I* knew he only needed that single thread of evidence.

Lennox. Think of a bottle; a pot-bellied, ridiculously-shaped bottle, then fill that bottle with cyanic acid. That was Lennox. That's how deadly he was. The man-hunter with the face and form of an overgrown cherub.

One part of me hated Lennox. Loathed his hail-fellow-well-met pitilessness. One part of me admired him, wished (strangely enough) that all policemen could be as ruthless, as incorruptible, as he was. But most of all I feared him.

I almost trembled as I recalled our conversation. Not what was said, but was implied – what was left *unsaid.* The subtle hints. The scarcely noticed nuances.

Lennox, I knew, would pin me. As surely and as easily as a cat might pin a wounded mouse.

Unless . . .

The beauty of the law, but at the same time the weak-ness of the law: evidence. And (again the beauty and the weakness) it would require a mass of evidence before the law would admit of a mistake. A mass of evidence. And – or so I hoped – not even Lennox could collect evidence enough to do more than level the scales of justice; to free Turnbull; to perhaps *know* the answer, but never to be able to *prove* the answer.

In this way I was to exorcise my ghosts.

I heard her first, heard her footsteps, but couldn't see her.

The footsteps were of a woman's shoes. They echoed slightly in the dark and for the moment deserted street. Their tempo told their own story. They were not hurrying. There was nothing deliberate about them; they were not the footsteps of a woman with a destination in mind.

They were dawdling. Strolling. Pausing now and again before moving slowly forward. They were the footsteps of a whore, plying her trade. A harlot offering herself to some passer-by.

I slowed to a halt, eased myself into a shadowed corner and watched. The street – it was Pervis Street – was quite deserted. Unlit except for the occasional backwash of some particularly strong and badly positioned headlights from a vehicle being driven along Lessford Road beyond the rows of buildings surrounding us. Quiet, too. Silent except for the distant murmur of that same traffic.

Later – in a few hours' time as midnight approached and the public houses disgorged their drunken customers – Pervis Street and all the other streets and alleys, all the other yards and closes, would be peopled by rowdies and oafs. But for the moment – probably for the next hour or so – nothing.

As always, the excitement rose within me. The satisfaction of knowing that another wrong was about to be righted; that one more portion of Sarah's life was about to be cancelled out. I flexed my gloved fingers in anticipation and stared along the unlit street.

The mind? You have my word that at such moments the mind achieves a peculiar clarity. It becomes fine-tuned to all possibilities and all probabilities. It bounds ahead of bodily functions, weighs pros and cons, calculates every risk, plans the right way, the easy way, the safe way.

Patrolling constables. I knew how many were on duty

in Bowling Side. I knew where they all were and I knew I had at least fifteen minutes before any one of them might come within screaming distance . . . assuming, of course, I muffed things and gave her a chance to scream.

If only I could *see* her.

I cleared my throat. A deliberate non-threatening noise with which to attract her attention. What murderer clears his throat at the sight of his victim? What victim sees danger in such an everyday sound?

She heard and she moved. No more than two steps . . . perhaps as she turned to see where the noise had come from. And knowing exactly where to look I saw her. A dark smudge against a black background.

I switched on my torch and strolled across. Quite deliberately I held the beam of the torch to show the outline of my uniform, the gleam of buttons on the tunic, the near-silhouette of 'officialdom'. So safe and reassuring. The one figure of which she need never be afraid.

She was I suppose about five foot nine or thereabouts. Trim figured. Bareheaded with mousey coloured hair cut 'urchin' style. Nothing outstanding, nothing beautiful, but at the same time nothing repulsive. She wore a raincoat – belted with the collar turned up – and over her right shoulder she carried a sling-style handbag. A very ordinary-looking woman. Walk down any thoroughfare – visit any supermarket – you will find dozens of similar women : similar that is except for one all-important and very obvious factor.

She was a street-walker.

The plastered cosmetics, the self-assured – almost contemptible – arrogance told their own story. The cheap perfume merely added olfactory verification.

'Working tonight, Inspector?' she murmured.

'You, too, it would seem.'

'Just – y'know – taking the air.' She smiled knowingly.

'A dangerous exercise these days,' I suggested.

'With you around?' The smile became more mocking.

'We were around before,' I reminded her. 'Walters, Hewitt, Golders. They too felt safe . . . presumably.'

'Very trusting,' she said and her lips curled into a sneer.

'But not you?'

'I don't trust a living soul, Inspector.'

'Wise,' I murmured.

'I'm a wise woman.'

'I'm glad.' Paused, then added, 'Did you know them?'

'Is it important?' she countered.

I wanted her off the street. There was a cul-de-sac, Fulcrum Court, about fifty yards away. That was where I wanted her. I moved slowly away as I continued the conversation.

I said, 'Everything's important. We're searching for a lead.'

'For whoever strangled Golders?' She moved into step with me as she asked the question.

'For whoever strangled them all,' I said.

'Turnbull.'

'No,' I shook my head. 'We now think not.'

'The poor bugger. Does *he* know?'

'Not yet.'

I clipped the torch to my uniform as I switched off the beam. I needed two hands. For the moment I thrust them into the pockets of my trousers.

She said, 'I thought the fuzz didn't make those sort of mistakes.'

'Sometimes,' I admitted. 'Not often.'

'Am I supposed to tell people?' she asked.

'What?'

'That Turnbull didn't kill Walters and Hewitt?'

'Don't spread it around too much,' I said. 'The wrong people might get to hear of it.'

'Turnbull for example?'

'He'll know soon enough,' I promised.

'That should make his day.'

'He'll be annoyed,' I sighed. 'But I think he'll understand.'

'He's that big a mug is he?' she mocked.

'He's a policeman.'

'*Is?*'

'Will be again,' I corrected myself.

My thoughts were busy. I had to get my hands up and beneath the fairly high collar of the raincoat. It was equally necessary that I get a thumb at each side of the windpipe and a good grip at the nape of the neck with my fingers. This meant us standing facing each other. It also meant speed. There must be no time for scratching and clawing, which in turn meant that my elbows must be spread outwards in order to deflect any sudden upward, defensive jerk of her hands.

This one, I decided *might* be a little more difficult than the other three. There was a peculiar self-assurance about her; a confidence the others had lacked.

Not that I doubted myself. I had the ability, there was ample proof of that. And, of course, I had a mission. An added mission, in fact, the proving of Turnbull's innocence.

I said, 'You knew the other three?'

'Walters, Hewitt and Golders?'

'You knew them?'

'*Of* them,' she said quietly.

'Really? I always thought you were a close-knit fraternity.'

'Some of us are loners.'

'Indeed? Despite Tomba Nayudu and his kind?'

'What I earn, I keep,' she said simply.

'Much?' I asked.

'That,' she said with a smile, 'is a very leading question.'

'True.'

This one, I decided, was a woman of some small intelligence. Not the normal mindless whore. A whore, of course, there was no doubt about *that*. But behind the plastered face and the inviting body there was a brain of sorts. Unlike the others she had made no promises. Offered no carnal fantasy. We might have been friends – at the very least acquaintances – strolling side-by-side and exchanging mildly humorous small talk.

Fulcrum Court was less than twenty yards away.

I said, 'You live in Bowling Side?'

'No.'

'I thought not. I – er – I know all the prostitutes of this area.'

'*All* of them?' For the first time innuendo touched the words.

A tiny spat of anger touched me as I said, 'Know them by name. Not by reputation.'

'Of course.' It was almost an apology.

'Your name?' I asked.

'There was,' she said dreamily, 'a lady who could do no wrong.'

'Messalina?'

'Above suspicion,' she murmured.

'Until . . .' I remarked gently.

'Until the eyes of Claudius were opened.'

She was, as I've already said, superior to any other harlot I'd ever met. In her own disgusting way a fascinating creature. A waste, perhaps, the waste of what might have been a good brain, but a waste deliberately chosen by herself.

I prepared the ground for the required turn into Fulcrum Court.

'You are,' I said, 'a woman of some perception.'

'A policeman *and* a flatterer?'

'Not flattery. Observation.'

She waited.

'Not Turnbull,' I said. 'Therefore somebody else.'

'It would seem,' she agreed.

'Somebody who vanishes at the sight of a police uniform. Somebody who perhaps *knows* policemen. Recognises them.'

'Their feet perhaps?' she smiled.

'I'm serious. We need help.'

'That I won't argue with.'

'Help us,' I said simply.

'How?'

'Look . . .' We'd reached the corner, I took her arm and guided her into the gloom of Fulcrum Court as I continued, 'Whoever he is he preys on people like you. Ladies of the street. That much is obvious.'

'Very obvious.'

We'd stopped walking. I turned, stood facing her and removed the other hand from my pocket.

I said, 'He hates your kind. Despises you. Kills whenever the opportunity presents itself. Therefore . . .'

My fingers flew at her throat: between the throat and the turned-up collar. My thumbs sought and found the carotid arteries at the base of her neck and, as I clenched my grip, I knew the blood-flow to the brain had ceased. Seconds – no more – and she'd be unconscious, then the strangulation proper could be performed. It would, I knew, be quite painless. The thought fortified me . . . I am not a cruel man.

There should have been terror. There was not terror. In

those few seconds, as the eyes began to glaze, there was, perhaps, apprehension, but, if so, only a hint of it. Triumph was there. Triumph in full and with it bottomless contempt.

As my fingers closed I held my arms ready to fend off the counter-attack. I tensed my muscles as I felt her hand move and I expected the nails to come clawing at my face. They didn't. Only her right hand moved and as she plunged it into my side I felt the knife being driven home hilt deep. Down there in the fleshy part below the ribs. I felt the blade bite hard and swift. And as consciousness left her she still continued to lean into me; holding the steel into position until the last moment then, as she went under, releasing her grasp in order that her weight might not tear the blade free.

The pain was less than I might have expected. It was there. I was under no illusion; I was wounded – probably mortally wounded – but instead of the sharp, snapping pain I might have expected, there was only an area of increasing heat. Heat which was burning me, burning me inside the guts, but, for the moment tolerable.

She had to die, of course. She *had* to die! She knew me, she could name me, therefore she *had* to die.

I forced myself to ignore the burning and tightened my grip on her throat. No mistake was acceptable. Even when I knew she was dead – even when she hung limp and lifeless from my aching arms – I continued the pressure. This one *had* to be dead and beyond all hope of recovery.

Nor had I time to leave the usual 'pointer'. The shoulder-bag would have been ideal but, apart from the growing pain, those last extra moments needed to ensure the certainty of death meant that the patrolling constable, due to pass the entrance of Fulcrum Court within the next five minutes, might be a little early and might . . .

147

The stupidity of it all! The lunacy of a mind coping at the same time with gathering pain and a crusading hatred of whoredom!

Of course they'd know it was me. This one – this 'Messalina' creature – had marked me as the killer. There was blood on her hand. My blood. There was blood on the hilt of the knife. And the blade of the knife was deep in my abdomen.

I was nailed.

Whether I left or whether I waited . . . I was nailed.

From darkness into light. Those words – that cliche – is the only manner in which to describe it. The knowledge of what I must do. The sudden clarity with which I saw the only logical ending.

I left the woman and slowly, painfully, walked the maze of streets towards my parked car. I knew the short cuts, I knew the shadowed alleys and I doubt if I passed more than four people.

As I walked, I debated. Whether or not to remove the knife. I decided to leave it in my flesh. There was blood, but not a gush of blood. A seeping. A steady run which in the main was being absorbed by my clothing. To withdraw the blade might have allowed the blood free flow. Therefore I padded a handkerchief, wrapped it around the hilt and held the knife hard home. By walking slowly and stiff-legged I was able to progress with tolerable pain.

Make no mistake. This was no act of heroism. But neither was it prompted by selfishness. I required Turnbull free. I was determined that whatever the dolts in a jury box might have said his absolute innocence had to be established. My killing of Elsie Golders while Turnbull was in prison had failed to reverse the verdict. It was possible – barely possible, but *just* possible – that this killing of the harlot who called herself 'Messalina' still might not be enough. The talk of 'carbon copy' murder was made too readily; the excuse via which the law's shortcomings could be brushed aside was still something which could not be dismissed.

Had I thought otherwise, had I been convinced that by staying with my latest victim fools like Harris and Warlock could have been made to acknowledge their mistake, I would have been content to remain and die at the scene. But because they were fools they might need more, therefore I had to *give* them more.

I reached the car. Carefully, gingerly – and not without extra agony – I lowered myself into the driver's seat.

The truth is I was becoming a little light-headed. My powers of concentration seemed to be on an elastic band. At some moments I enjoyed complete lucidity. At others the world seemed a vague and spinning place. But most of the time I stayed in the grey area between; a conscious effort was required before each movement was attempted and completed.

I rested in the car still holding the blade in position at my left side.

How long?

God knows. At times like that consciousness – life itself – resembles a cinematograph film without the necessary projector : viewed frame at a time and almost at a standstill. Time is seen for what it really is. An illusion. A man-made measurement of infinity, therefore ridiculous. perhaps it increased slowly. I have no real means of knowing. It seemed to accelerate; to drive itself into the lower part of my body more sharply with each intake of breath; to start a furnace somewhere below the navel, then fan the furnace until it was white hot and almost unbearable.

The car radio sent out my call sign.

'Control calling zero-five-one. Control calling zero-five-one.'

I glanced at the speaker, but didn't answer the call.

'Control calling zero-five-one. Come in, please.'

Such a stupid request! I was there. I *knew*. The body of the woman had been found, that was the obvious and only excuse for the breathless urgency of the policewoman calling over the radio waves. I needn't 'come in'. I needn't be told. I needn't even listen.

I twisted my body, sucked in air as the movement ripped more pain into me and, still keeping my left hand on the knife handle, reached across and switched off the radio.

Gently, one-handed, I started the engine, released the hand-brake and drove at a slow cruising speed. Carefully. Forcing myself to ignore the gathering pain. It is possible to drive one-handed while at the same time holding the left hand tight against the lower part of the rib cage. It is difficult, but it is possible. I drove in third gear; a gear which didn't threaten to stall the engine as I timed the traffic lights to arrive at the green; not to have to brake and not to have to use the clutch pedal with my left foot. Not a nightmare journey. That would be an exaggeration. But a journey I would not like to repeat.

I crawled into the car park at the rear of Bowling Side Police Station and eased the car into the white-lined rectangle reserved for my use. I stopped the car; I stopped it by merely switching off the ignition. Then I switched off the lights, sat there and deliberately fought the pain.

This is possible. With practice it becomes comparatively easy. Pain – all pain, mental pain and physical pain – can with will-power become almost a companion. The trick, if it can be rightly called a 'trick', is to accept the pain as part of the whole; to ignore it as something extra and instead embrace it until it becomes akin to an extra

150

limb. Its throb is in rhythm with the heart beat, therefore allow it to *be* part of the heart beat. As with all hurts, to ignore it diminishes its power to dominate.

I speak as an expert. I have had years of practise.

When I was certain the rear of the police station was deserted, I eased myself from the car and walked slowly to the door leading to the cell passage. The door was still unlocked; what prisoners the night might yet bring had not been arrested. From there I limped my way up the rear stairs, step at a time and reached the empty Incident Centre.

That, of course, is where I am now. Recording this story on to cassettes. The whole story. What happened. Why it happened . . . and why I *made* it happen.

There must, of course, be motive.

Means, opportunity and motive. The three pillars upon which men like Harris, men like Warlock, construct every criminal prosecution. Motive to such narrow-minded men is of supreme importance. Why? Is it not enough that a man kills? Is the killing itself not sufficient? Must they also have a handy peg upon which they might hang a reason – a reason *they* can understand?

It would seem so. Otherwise Turnbull would not now be in prison.

My apologies to Turnbull. The 'pointers' – the shoe, the mac, the glove – were there for a purpose. As section inspector I knew when policemen would pass the scene. I timed it well. I desired a policeman to discover the body. A policeman – not a civilian – if only because a civilian without an alibi might find himself wrongly accused. The conviction of an innocent was not part of my scheme.

I reckoned without the pig-headed stupidity of Warlock and Harris. I reckoned without the human weakness of Constable Turnbull. However careful the planning nobody can bypass mulish obstinacy and the carnality of a harlot's temptations. No, not even when I demonstrated, via the glove, that Warlock himself could be made to 'find' a newly murdered trollop. It was wasted. With oafs like Warlock subtleties are *always* wasted.

However . . . motive.

To rid the world of whores? That I know sounds ridiculous. The ravings of an unhinged mind. But – to fall back on cliches – every journey starts with a first step. To rid *Bowling Side* of whores. That would be something. For seven years they have disgusted me. For seven years they've sauntered the streets of *my* police section, and the law has winked its eye and turned its other cheek.

The object, then, was to go beyond the law. To invoke Natural Law. The law of common decency. To rid an area – *my* area – of vermin – via fear.

My estimation was very conservative. Less than a dozen . . . that was the calculation upon which I worked. Less than a dozen dead harlots and the district would become decent. Death can be a great argument. And if the street-women of Bowling Side had once become convinced that their profession carried within it the seeds of strangulation they would have changed their ways, that or moved out.

Such a small price to pay in order to rid a district of vermin. The whores and those who batten on whores: like clearing the rats from an old drainage system. It *can* be done. It must and should be done.

I have failed, but at least I have shown the way. The only way. This so-called 'oldest profession' – this pandering for lust, pornography and lewdness – it is *not* 'natural'. That argument is utterly invalid. The beasts of the world do not indulge themselves in this manner. We, the humans, are the only species whose females copulate for personal gain.

We are foul. Disgusting. And if I have shown the way

152

– if some other person more fortunate than I succeeds where I have failed – I die a contented man.

I should, I suppose, put my house in order.

So be it. The pain is gradually taking over. Fortunately, I have been granted enough privacy here in this Incident Centre to tell the whole story without being interrupted.

For the benefit of Her Majesty's Coroner therefore . . .

I am of a sound mind. I am at this moment in full control of all my senses. I have been knifed by a woman whose working name is 'Messalina'. I in turn killed her via manual strangulation. I also killed Emilia Walters. And Bertha Hewitt. And Elsie Golders. All by means of manual strangulation.

I have no regrets.

My only regret is that I have been unable to end what I set out to do.

On a personal level . . .

The house – the house whose mortgage I cleared after Father died and which is now my property – this I leave to Aunt Elizabeth to do with as she wishes. The same with whatever money or goods I own. All to go to Aunt Elizabeth. Nothing to go to Mother, other than by the wishes of Aunt Elizabeth.

In this I clear two debts. The debt to Aunt Elizabeth for the endless kindness and understanding she has always shown to me. The debt to Mother for the equally endless bickering and selfishness . . . plus the undoubted fact that her impossible demands drove Sarah away from me.

And to my colleagues in the force?

A detestation, amounting to near-hatred, for Warlock and his inbred bigotry. An utter contempt for Harris, for his arrogance and the manner in which he dismisses all opinions other than his own.

For Chris Tallboy I feel sadness. He was, I think, the

153

only man I could ever call 'friend'. He was the only truly happy man I ever met and for this I envied him greatly.

I thank him for trying to share some of that happiness with a man who, it would seem, was incapable of receiving it.

SEVEN

The speaker hissed quietly as the unused tape was fed through the machine. Lennox leaned forward, pressed the 'Stop' button and the spools of the cassette stopped turning.

'And that's it.' Lennox settled back in his chair. 'That's where he flaked out. That's the whole story.'

'Not quite,' said Harris grimly. 'He was unlucky. He didn't die, and from what the medics say he'll live.'

Tallboy cleared his throat, but remained silent.

They were in Gilliant's office. The four of them; Gilliant, Harris, Lennox and Tallboy. They'd listened in silence as Caan's voice had come over the speaker; as Lennox had fed each cassette into the play-back machine. Each man had hidden his thoughts behind a stone-faced expression.

Gilliant's tone was almost accusatory as he said, 'You seemed to know, Mr Lennox. That last time you spoke to him in the Incident Centre. If what he says is to be believed you'd already guessed.'

'A long shot, sir.' Lennox's podgy face screwed itself into a worried frown. 'One o' those stabs in the dark.'

'It can be argued that you might have prevented the fourth murder.'

'If you say so,' grunted Lennox.

'And what would *you* say?' asked Gilliant softly.

'I'd say you were talking cock, sir, with respect.'

'Don't overdo the "respect", Chief Superintendent,' said Gilliant warningly.

'A blinder.' There was soft but savage rage in the fat detective's tone. 'It could have been anybody. Any copper. Aye . . . even Warlock. Any of 'em. That's the way the straw seemed to be bending. It seemed possible. If not Turnbull, why not some other copper?'

'You sound as if you were ,sure it *wasn't* Turnbull.' Harris's eyes glinted.

'At that time? I was pretty bloody sure.'

'You kept your opinion very much to yourself.'

Lennox rumbled, 'Would it have helped? Caan's right in that respect.'

'Caan's a self-confessed multiple murderer,' snapped Harris.

'Aye.' Lennox nodded ponderously. 'And like the chief you think I sent him out to do that last killing.'

'Didn't you?'

'No!' Lennox matched rage for rage. 'I trusted him. He'd dropped enough hints that he thought Turnbull was innocent. I needed eyes and ears inside Bowling Side.'

'Some eyes and ears,' sneered Harris.

'Lookee.' Lennox thrust his chin forward. 'You've maybe known more murderers than I have, but I've known a few. How many of 'em have worried because some innocent sod was doing time for *their* killings?'

'That's a damn poor excuse.'

'It is *now.*'

'Inspector Tallboy?' Gilliant's question was a little like a curtain drawn between two charging bulls. He said, 'You were his friend. Your opinion might be worth listening to.'

'He was sure of Turnbull's innocence.' Tallboy's throat was dry. His voice low and a little hoarse. 'Obviously he was sure, but that's not what I'm getting at. He wanted everybody else to be sure. I – I think his conscience was too big to handle. The women? I don't know. Some psychiatrist might work that out. But to him his victim – his *only* victim – was Constable Turnbull.'

*

Some miles away in a tiny, single-bed ward at Kemington Royal Infirmary the subject of their conversation moved in and away from consciousness, much as a piece of floating debris washes against a beach before being pulled back by the underflow of an incoming tide.

A detective constable sat on a chair by the bed; a stolid, unemotional man, a man happy to glance through the contents of a two-week-old glossy magazine without reading it and without being too much interested in its articles and stories. To him the Bowling Side murders were at an end. Life could now revert back to normality, the lesser crimes could be reported, the snouts could be visited and leaned upon a little, the miserable little snotrag who'd nicked this or pinched the other could be collared, and every monthly pay cheque saw so many more weeks nearer to a pension.

His instructions had been simple and specific. Listen, note and say as little as possible.

A man not soured, but rather made immune to the feelings of others by reason of his profession. Not a hard man, not a cruel man, but a man who viewed friendship with suspicion. The perfect choice for this particular detail.

The door of the tiny ward opened and a white-coated doctor accompanied by a middle-aged nurse entered. The detective constable lowered the magazine and made as if to raise from the chair.

'It's all right, officer.' The doctor waved the D.C. to remain seated.

The nurse and doctor stood at each side of the bed and examined the unconscious patient.

'About another hour,' murmured the doctor.

'No liquids, of course?' The nurse raised her voice slightly on the last two words and made it a question.

'He'll ask for a drink. Moisten his lips, no more. Perhaps

157

tomorrow.'

The nurse nodded her understanding.

'Keep an eye on the dressing. And let me know if his temperature starts to rise or if his pulse-rate fluctuates more than might be expected.'

'Yes, Doctor.'

'He should be okay.' The doctor's expression relaxed into a quick smile. 'A healthy man, Nurse. He saved his own life by holding the knife in position.'

In their own way they were as impersonal as the detective constable. The unconscious man was to them a 'success'; without the skill of them and their kind he might be dead; without their continued skill he might still die, but every hour of life increased the certainty of his survival.

None of the three people in the tiny ward consciously thought of the man as a multiple murderer. To two of them he was primarily a patient. To the third he was a prisoner, and one more mug.

'Those.' Gilliant nodded at the cassettes. 'They're inadmissible as evidence.'

'For God's sake . . .' began Harris.

'There's more than one court ruling,' insisted Gilliant.

'The Moors Murder job.' Harris refused to be defeated without an argument.

'Not from the accused,' growled Lennox. '*Made* by the accused . . . proof of the commission of the crime. There's a difference.'

'It's a dying declaration for God's sake,' said Harris.

'That,' said Gilliant drily, 'is an argument I, for one, wouldn't like to put up in a Crown Court.'

'He thought he was dying. Dammit he *expected* to die.'

'He was alone. He spoke into a machine. He's a layman,

158

no medic had told him he was a gonner. He equated pain with death. It won't wash, Mr Harris. We still need proof . . . *real* proof.'

'All right!' Harris's face coloured. 'All that yammering into a microphone. I'll have it done in black and white. Every word typed. Then the bastard can sign it. *That'll* . . .'

'After you've cautioned him,' interrupted Lennox.

'Eh?'

Lennox's tone carried weary disgust as he said, 'Harris, old cock. Typing it out doesn't mean a damn thing . . . *and* you know it. The tapes are inadmissible. A transcript of the tapes is inadmissible – even *more* inadmissible. It's one more step removed from the real thing. Maybe he'll sign, maybe he won't. But before he even reads the transcript he'll have to be formally cautioned. That's an admission of four killings, boy. It's other things, too. Never mind what he says at the end. You get a good wig-and-gown lad defending and that little lot makes one hell of a foundation for a plea of insanity.'

'Jesus wept!' exploded Harris. 'Doesn't *anybody* in this office want to put the hound where he belongs?'

'You do.' Tallboy's voice was hard. Brittle with controlled rage. He said, 'Where *you* think he belongs. Behind bars for the rest of his life. In a hanging-shed if topping was still in vogue. You want to do to him what *he* did to the women, and for the same mad reason. He's innocent. He's . . .'

'The hell he's innocent!'

'He's innocent until a jury decides otherwise. And *you're* not the judge and *you're* not the jury. Those cassettes don't make him guilty. A transcript doesn't make him guilty And – dammit – *you* don't make him guilty. This lot. This discussion . . .' Tallboy waved a hand slightly. 'It's a re-run of the Turnbull thing. You were so sure then. So infernally *sure*. And so bloody *wrong*. You heard the tapes . . . you heard 'em, but did you listen to 'em? What they tried to say but couldn't? When he gets to know . . .'

'He'll get to know.' Harris's voice was almost a shout. 'I, personally, will take great pleasure in . . .'

Gilliant snapped, 'You're off the case, Mr Harris.'

'*What*?'

'You're off the case,' repeated Gilliant. 'You're far too emotionally involved.'

'Like hell I'm off the case. Nobody can . . .'

'*I can.*' Suddenly the three other men knew exactly why Gilliant had been made chief constable. It was there in the bitingly cold tone; in the absolute authority; in the two words which slammed a door in Harris's face. Gilliant continued, 'You are off the case, Mr Harris. Concentrate on other crime. Chief Superintendent Lennox is in sole charge of the case against Caan. And – understand this – if I as much as hear of you even discussing the Caan affair with *anybody* I won't wait for your resignation. That's all, Mr Harris. Leave us, please.'

As the medics had prophesied Caan recovered. Within a week he was on a liquid diet and within ten days he was on carefully chosen solids. His world was encompassed by the walls of the cell-like ward and he was never left alone. Nevertheless Lennox chose his guards well; quiet men, compassionate men, men ready and willing to treat Caan with more than superficial sympathy. Men who let Caan himself set the pace; men who were prepared to talk if Caan wanted to talk or, equally, were prepared to remain silent if Caan preferred silence.

Lennox visited the prisoner immediately the medical experts had given an assurance that Caan had recovered sufficiently to fully understand what was being said to him. Lennox sent the guard out of the tiny ward, settled his bulk on to the chair and favoured the man in the bed with a lop-sided grin.

'Off the record, Caan, old son.'

'It doesn't have to be.'

'I know, but it *is*.'

Caan nodded.

'You need a solicitor. What the hell you feel like now doesn't matter. The dawn'll break when you'll wish you'd asked for a solicitor. Get one.'

'Perhaps.'

'Ask him to have a word with me before he sees you . . . eh?'

'I'll tell him.'

'Meanwhile – y'know – take it day at a time. Try not to worry too much.'

'Turnbull?' asked Caan gently.

Lennox said, 'It takes time, son. The papers are being prepared – that's the expression ain't it? They'll be at the Home Office within the next few days. Then he'll be a free man.'

'Before the trial?'

'It – er – it seems likely.'

'I hope so.'

'Aye. So do I.' Lennox switched subject and said, 'No newspapers – that's orders from the chief – but magazines, books, that sorta thing.'

'I'm all right.'

'Just ask. That's all.'

'Thanks.' Caan hesitated, then added, 'Thanks for everything.'

'Hey.' The lop-sided grin came and went once more. 'We're on opposite sides, old son. Don't forget that.'

And each day Caan grew a little stronger and each

day a little more morose. It was as if, with the gradual return of health, the enormity of his crimes became more apparent. As his bodily health improved, his mental health seemed to deteriorate. The men who sat guard on him did their best; newspapers, television and radio were forbidden, but within carefully prescribed limits they brought news of the outside world. Sometimes Caan listened, asked questions and seemed interested. At other times he sat up in bed and stared, unseeing, at the wall of the ward; not hearing, not answering, seemingly not aware. On at least one occasion tears spilled from his eyes and flowed unheeded down his cheeks.

Tallboy visited him twice – sometimes three times – each week. He brought paperbacks and cigarettes and on one occasion, after leaving Caan in a mood of black depression, he sought the advice of the hospital psychiatrist.

'What happens when we tell him?'

'You're asking an impossible question, Inspector.'

The psychiatrist was a solemn-faced man, bearded and balding, a man wise enough to know that certainty in *his* branch of medicine was a form of foolishness. They talked in the psychiatrist's office and as they talked they sipped tea, munched biscuits and smoked cigarettes.

'He'll *have* to be told,' said Tallboy.

'Of course.'

'He – er . . .' Tallboy paused, then said, 'What's wrong with him, Doctor? I don't mean the stab wound. I mean his manner. He's not the same man.'

'He's committed four murders,' said the psychiatrist simply. 'He's just beginning to realise that.'

'You mean . . . he didn't know before?'

'Before,' said the psychiatrist slowly, 'it was a form of crusade. You've heard the tapes?'

'Naturally.'

'That's a fanatic speaking. The first two killings . . . a fanatic, intent upon cleaning the world of an evil. The second two? The same fanaticism. But this time also to clear the name of an innocent man.'

'He was . . . mad?' Hope hung by the fingertips to the question.

'Depends what you mean by "mad".' The psychiatrist spoke slowly and carefully. 'Legally insane? No. He knew he was committing murder. He knew murder was a crime. Legally he was – still is – as sane as you or I. Medically insane? Well now, that takes some answering. *Was* he? At the time of the killings, I mean. Is *any* fanatic fully sane? I'd say not. Fanaticism itself being a form of mental imbalance. This pathological hatred of prostitutes . . . further proof of an unstable mind. You can dislike them, you can disapprove of them, but unless there's something seriously wrong with your mind you don't go around killing them. In layman's language that's what it boils down to. And I'm prepared to stand up in court and say just that, but no more.

'The reasons for this mental instability for example. Given time – and by that I mean months, probably years – I might be able to give an adequate answer. I *might*. The glib answer is because his sister left him and because they were so close. Equally because he's mother-dominated and lived in a world of old-fashioned females. But . . .' The psychiatrist sighed. 'The hell of it is we know so little. You can *see* a broken leg. You can see where it's broken and how bad the break is. You can ask and you'll be told exactly *what* broke the bone. With a broken mind? You can't see it . . . only the consequences of it. You can't see where it's broken, you can't see how badly it's broken and as for finding out *how* it was broken? It doesn't snap, y'see, Inspector. In that respect it's not like a bone. It takes pressure. Tremendous pressure sometimes. And sometimes it isn't even aware of that pressure. Then one day it goes, and externally that day is no different to any other day.'

They both remained silent for a few moments. Sad moments; moments without hope.

'And now?' asked Tallboy softly. 'Today?'

Once more the psychiatrist spoke slowly and carefully; wanting to help, wanting to explain, but unwilling to commit himself beyond the point where knowledge ended and guesswork began.

He said, 'The original break is mending. Let's take that as a working hypothesis. That original break – the break which created the fanaticism – is healing, has almost healed. That means he knows what he is. What he *really* is. A multiple murderer. A man whose crime sent an innocent man to prison.'

'Why should it heal?' asked Tallboy. 'Why? At this particular moment?'

'If you'd had a knife driven into your lower abdomen . . .' The psychiatrist's lips twisted for a moment. 'Physical pain, Inspector. It doesn't stop there. It *never* stops there. Pain equates with the nervous system. The nervous system equates with the mind. Severe physical pain reflects itself upon the mind . . . always! It causes an imbalance, how-ever slight that imbalance. But if the imbalance is already *there*. In that case, equally, it can sometimes balance the *im*balance. That's putting it very crudely, but that's what it adds up to.'

Tallboy nodded his understanding.

'Follow the hypothesis through,' continued the psychia-trist. 'We have Caan confronted by something very frightening . . . the knowledge of himself as a multiple murderer. One break mends. But at what fresh pressure!'

'Another break? A different break?'

'It happens . . . too often for comfort. It's happening with Caan.'

'And when he gets to know the truth?' asked Tallboy.

'Guess. Your guess will be as good as mine.'

'And *your* guess?'

'One of two things.' The psychiatrist frowned. 'He could close a door. Reject it. Refuse to accept it as a fact.'

'Or?'

'My friend put bluntly it could be rather like pushing a stick of dynamite into one of his ears then lighting the fuse. It *could* blow his mind to shreds.'

In seven weeks the file was almost ready for presentation : the statements had all been taken; the forensic scientists had forged their chain of immaculate evidence; the various medical opinions had all been recorded; the Police Prosecuting Solicitor had examined the file for possible faults or weaknesses and found none.

That gentleman – along with Lennox and Tallboy – was in Gilliant's office holding a final conference prior to committal proceedings at Bordfield Magistrates' Court.

There was one tiny fly in the forensic ointment. All four men knew of it and the P.P.S. was merely reminding them.

'He hasn't yet been arrested. He hasn't yet been cautioned and charged with the offences. I know why . . .' The solicitor brushed aside Lennox's attempt to interrupt. He added, 'At least I *think* I know why. I can only hope his own solicitor shares our views.'

'Why shouldn't he?' asked Gilliant.

'It can be argued that it weakens our case. That if we'd been so sure we'd have gone through the normal formalities. Arrest. Charge. Then perhaps bail until the case could be heard.'

'*Perhaps* bail,' grunted Lennox.

'We wouldn't have opposed it in the circumstances,' said the P.P.S.

'We couldn't have been sure.'

'Agreed. But . . .'

'Let's assume he *hadn't* got bail.' Lennox eyed the solicitor quizzically. 'What then?'

'Prison hospital.'

'Aye.' Lennox nodded. 'Well, that's where he is now in effect. Has been since we found him unconscious in the Incident Centre. In hospital under guard. Same thing, but a little more humane. We all agree he's a sick man. Shoving him in clink – even in hospital clink – wouldn't have helped.'

'He hasn't yet been charged,' insisted the P.P.S. 'That's most irregular.'

'That's another reason. A big reason. When he's . . .'

'*I'm* charging him this evening.' Tallboy spoke for the first time. 'I'm charging him. I'm cautioning him. I'm inviting him to sign a transcript of those tapes. Which means I'm *telling* him.' He sighed, then added, 'I wish to hell I wasn't.'

'You're his friend,' said Gilliant. 'From you it might be acceptable.'

The P.P.S. said, 'Acceptable or not, it has to be *accepted*.'

'Ten days ago . . .' Tallboy took a deep breath. 'Ten days ago his sister visited him. Sarah, his sister. I was there. It's something I won't forget in a hurry.'

She was such a very ordinary person; medium height, medium build, medium everything. As he walked alongside her Tallboy wondered what the hell there was about the woman which caused such anguish of mind in her brother. Even her personality – even her voice – seemed

166

somehow 'mass-produced'. Dammit even her clothes. Even her hair-style.

He murmured, 'He's a sick man, Miss Caan.'

'So I understand.'

'You know what you *mustn't* tell him?'

'I've been warned. I don't see why not.'

'Because he's a sick man.'

'Inspector,' she asked, 'is he "sick" because he's murdered four women?'

'The other way round,' said Tallboy. 'He killed *because* he was sick.'

'Those four dead women,' she mused. 'I'll bet **they** wish *they* were only "sick".'

There was no reasonable answer to that one, therefore Tallboy didn't even try. He walked with the woman along the corridors of the hospital and tried to work out the possible ways in which the coming meeting might screw things up beyond all hope.

He opened the door of the tiny ward, moved his head as a sign of dismissal to the detective constable sitting guard, then closed the door behind the D.C. and joined the woman at the bedside.

Caan was staring at her.

'Eddie,' she said softly.

Caan moved his eyes to Tallboy's face and asked a silent question.

'It's Sarah,' said Tallboy. 'It's your sister.'

Caan glanced at the woman, then returned his gaze to Tallboy and grinned an idiot's grin.

'It's Sarah,' insisted Tallboy.

Caan gazed at the woman in silence for a few moments, then said, 'It *is*?'

'It's me, Eddie,' she assured him.

'You were once beautiful,' said Caan.

'No.' She shook her head. 'Like I am now . . . a few years younger.'

'Beautiful,' repeated Caan.

'Is he drugged?' She asked the question of Tallboy.

'Something.' Tallboy moved his shoulders. 'It quietens him. Stops him from weeping.'

She returned her attention to the man in the bed.

'What made you do it, Eddie?' she asked.

'Easy,' murmured Tallboy.

Caan's face changed. Recognition arrived and with it a release of tightly held emotion; an explosion of loathing and accusation, which brought tiny bubbles of spittle to the corners of the mouth.

'You made me do it. You!' Caan's voice rose and fell as he hurled insults at the white-faced woman. 'You walked out on me. You left me alone with that bitch. You – you turned *rotten*. Unclean. Vile. You showed me what you were. A cow. A selfish, dirty-minded cow! Every time I killed it was *you* I was killing. *Your* throat was there under my fingers. *You* were the one. Always *you*.'

'Easy, Eddie.' Tallboy moved nearer to the bed.

'Don't you see her?' Caan turned to Tallboy for confirmation of his sick rage. 'Can't you see what she is? How ugly it's made her? Whoredom. It has that effect. The filth shows. It destroys all beauty. She used to be beautiful, Chris. Beautiful! My God . . . look at her now. A tart pretending to be respectable. A whore making believe . . .'

'That's enough!' Tallboy shouted the raving Caan down. He turned to the woman and in a quieter tone said, 'You too, miss. That's enough. I think you'd better leave.'

She nodded dumbly.

In the bed Caan's face seemed to crumble and tears streamed down his cheeks.

Tallboy guided the stunned woman to the door of the ward and into the corridor. He spoke to the waiting detective constable.

'Inside. Sit with him. Quieten him down as much as you can. I'll have somebody along to see him as soon as possible.'

Gilliant said, 'I'll not make it an order, Inspector. Nevertheless I'd like you to volunteer. He accepts you as his friend. He has to *be* charged, it might be kinder if it came from you.'

'I'll be present as witness,' suggested Lennox.

'I'll do it,' muttered Tallboy. 'Of course I'll do it, and I'd like you there, Mr Lennox.'

'His own solicitor?' asked the Police Prosecuting Solicitor.

Gilliant said, 'He's been notified. There's a "Guilty" plea . . . he's heard the tapes and read the transcript. To use his own phrase he can "see no useful purpose" in being present.'

The P.P.S. frowned his annoyance.

Lennox growled, 'Some of 'em get their money the easy way.'

'Nevertheless,' said Gilliant, 'it shows a degree of trust. Give him the benefit of the doubt. Look at it in that light.'

'Six-thirty suit?' asked Lennox.

'Fine.' Tallboy nodded. 'I'll have a word with the psychiatrist. Make sure his mind's as clear as possible.'

There followed a little desultory conversation; a checking of facts and a deciding upon of minor points concerning the presentation of what little evidence might be required. They left Gilliant's office at a little after four o'clock; the P.P.S. to his own office in order to put the finishing touches to a case which on the face of things would need little or no forensic skill; Lennox to his home for a quick snack prior to his meeting with Tallboy; Tallboy to the nearest telephone in order to notify the hospital psychiatrist of the evening's visit to Caan.

Caan seemed remarkably balanced. There was perhaps a gleam in his eyes, but it might have been the gleam of contented anticipation, rather than of pick-me-up dope. He seemed calm. Resigned. Almost happy at the prospect of ending this wait for what he must have known was the inevitable. He was sitting up in bed spruced and wearing freshly laundered pyjamas under a silk dressing-gown.

Having dismissed the detective constable doing guard duty, Tallboy seated himself in the chair and waited until Lennox had made himself comfortable at the foot of the bed. Tallboy had a slim briefcase on his knees and he spoke as he flipped the snap fasteners open.

'You know why we're here, Eddie?'

'Of course.' Caan smiled.

'You have to be charged. Charged with murder. But first you have to be cautioned.'

'That isn't necessary,' smiled Caan. 'I know my rights.'

Lennox murmured, 'Caution him, Tallboy. We've cut enough corners on this one.'

Tallboy cleared his throat and said, 'Edmund Caan, it is my duty to warn you that you are not obliged to say anything unless you wish to do so. It is also my duty to warn you that whatever you say may be taken down in writing and used in evidence.'

Caan nodded, then solemnly said, 'I murdered Emilia Walters. I also murdered Bertha Hewitt. I also murdered Elsie Golders. I also murdered a woman whose name I don't know, but who was prostituting herself under the name of "Messalina". I killed them all by manual strangulation.'

There was a silence.

Then Caan looked at Tallboy and said, 'Is that enough?'

'If you say so,' said Tallboy.

As Tallboy opened the briefcase, Caan spoke to Lennox. He said, 'Turnbull . . . is he free yet?'

'Not yet, old son.'

'But that's ridiculous. I've already . . .'

'The law,' sighed the fat detective. 'It finds you "Guilty". It automatically releases Turnbull. But it has to *find* you "Guilty" . . . see? Otherwise any crackpot could stroll up and admit a crime and some lad inside could walk free. It makes sense, old son. A few days more, that's all.'

'I intend to plead "Guilty".'

'Aye.' Lennox bobbed his head. 'Your solicitor said so.'

'The sooner I go on trial the better then?'

'Aye.' Again Lennox nodded.

'That – that taped confession . . .' A vertical furrow folded the skin between Caan's eyes.

'Inadmissible evidence,' said Tallboy brusquely.

'Oh!'

'This.' Tallboy lifted a clipped file of foolscap from the briefcase. 'A typescript of what you said. It's headed by the Official Caution . . . a sort of voluntary statement. It'll carry more weight than the tapes. I'd like you to . . .'

'I'll sign it.' Caan answered before the request was made.

'Read it,' said Tallboy.

'I trust you. I'll sign it. I want Turnbull out of prison as soon as possible.'

'Read it, Eddie,' insisted Tallboy. 'All of it. Then – if you wish and if you agree with what it says – sign the caution, initial each sheet and sign your name and date at the bottom.'

He handed the typescript and a ballpoint to the man in the bed, then he rose from the chair, pushed his hands deep into the pockets of his trousers and walked slowly to the small-paned window of the tiny ward. He stood and stared through the window at the lighted wards across a rectangle of muddy lawn. As he spoke his head remained still. His eyes continued to stare unseeing at the opposite wards. His voice was low and gentle.

He said, 'The charges, Eddie. Four murders. Walters, Hewitt, Golders and the woman who called herself "Messalina". You – er – you built up quite a crime wave. Terrified everybody . . . the Bowling Siders, I mean.'

'Turnbull.' Caan had hardly glanced at the typed foolscap. 'Those last two. It was for him, you know. For Turnbull. I had to show how mad it had been to convict an innocent man. I mean . . .'

'The vigilante groups.' Tallboy imposed his voice over that of the man in the bed. He spoke a little louder. With the hint of authority. He continued to stare at the window as he continued, 'Illegal, of course. But a lot of people wanted you caught. You – er – realise that, of course?'

'Of course.' Caan sounded amazed – even annoyed – at the basic stupidity of the question.

'Including the woman,' said Tallboy gently.

'Which woman?'

'The woman who knifed you. She – er – set herself up as a target.'

'Oh!'

'That's er . . .' Tallboy seemed at loss for words.

Caan chuckled quietly and said, 'We both won, but we both lost.'

' "Messalina".' Tallboy seemed to groan the word. 'She wasn't even a whore. It was – it was . . . *Turnbull's wife.*'

Tallboy turned in time to see Lennox throw the full

172

weight of his body across the man who was trying to scramble from the bed and reach Tallboy's throat with clawed fingers. There was madness in Caan's expression, complete and absolute madness.

Tallboy hurled himself to the assistance of the fat detective and at the same time yelled for help.

'Like pushing a stick of dynamite into one of his ears then lighting the fuse.' Tallboy's hand trembled slightly as he lifted the cigarette to his mouth. He exhaled smoke then said, 'That was one hell of an appropriate description.'

'The odds were all in favour, Inspector.' The psychiatrist was a pipe-man. He flicked a king-sized lighter and directed the tongue of what appeared to be a miniaturised flame-thrower on to what little tobacco remained in the bowl of his pipe. Between puffs he said, 'Some things we're not too sure about. But Caan . . . I'd had time enough to form an opinion. There was no easy way. However hard you tried, there was no easy way.'

Lennox growled, 'You did your best, old son. You led him to it as easily as possible, but eventually you had to hit him with it.'

Lennox also was smoking; a thin, evil-smelling cheroot.

The psychiatrist's office was thick with whirls and spirals of tobacco smoke. It seemed appropriate. The fog of the atmosphere seemed to approximate the unknown quality of the human mind under stress.

'How long?' asked Tallboy.

'Before he's better? Before he's rational?' The psychiatrist waved his pipe in a hopeless, helpless gesture. 'Years . . . if ever.'

'For God's sake!'

'That's only an opinion.' The psychiatrist's tone had the edge of the expert whose knowledge was being doubted. 'I'm not God. I don't know everything. But this

I *do* know – this I'll stake my professional reputation on – the Edmund Caan you knew no longer exists. The law demanded that he be told the truth, and the truth destroyed him.'

'I'm sorry,' apologised Tallboy.

'Y'see, Doc.' Lennox eased the tension by reducing intricacies until they were simple statements of fact. 'Y'see,' he rumbled, 'Caan never got round to signing that transcript . . . assuming that might have helped matters. The tapes ain't evidence. And if I understand you right poor old Caan isn't going to be in a fit condition to plead, even assuming we're daft enough to shove him in a dock.'

'He's totally unfit to plead,' agreed the psychiatrist.

'And that,' sighed Lennox, 'is what's griping young Tallboy here. The law ain't perfect, but it's certain. One o' those merry, Christmas-cracker mottoes the judges trot out every now and again. "Better to have a bad law than an uncertain law". Well that's *their* opinion. But if it's "certain" that means it doesn't make mistakes. And on the few occasions it *does* make a mistake it ain't too keen to admit it. But – y'see – if Caan had stood trial for all four killings that would have meant the law *had* made a mistake . . . Caan being very anxious to plead "Guilty" and let Turnbull off the hook. But now . . .' Lennox screwed his face into a frown 'God only knows. Officially, we're left with two undetected murders. But more than that, officially Turnbull's left holding a very nasty baby . . . the lawful conviction of two murders he didn't commit. I dunno. Maybe we can get the Home Secretary to do his tricks. But what do you think?' Lennox spread his hands. 'The taped voice of a crazy man – that's what it boils down to. It ain't much, Doc. I doubt if it's enough.'

THE ENDING

Take the west road from London; travel through the Berkshire commuter belt of Maidenhead, Windsor and Staines; continue to Bracknell, then on to Crowthorne. And there you will find it. Probably the best, certainly the most well-known, criminal lunatic asylum in the world.

Broadmoor.

You can see nothing; the mile-long surrounding wall ensures both privacy and security. But inside that wall along with all the necessary administative, workshop and hospital facilities, there are three-storey 'blocks'. There are seven such 'blocks', and Block Six is perhaps the most feared block of all. Block Six is the only maximum security block, and within it prisoners ('patients' as they are more rightly called) who are given to excess violence and who are severely ill are housed and cared for. By the very nature of Broadmoor – and the people who run it – hope is never completely abandoned, but very little hope remains for the inmates of Block Six.

One such inmate recognises nobody. He doesn't even remember his own name. His mind races from horror to horror; a torture chamber locked inside his own skull and eased only temporarily by massive doses of quietening drugs.

About two hundred miles north of this tormented man there is another man serving out a 'life' sentence in a more conventional prison. He remains there despite committees and action groups and pleas by Members of Parliament.

This man is quite innocent, but that is of little importance.

The law, it seems, must continue to be 'certain' . . . even when it is *wrong*.